ESSENCE

ESSENCE EXTRACTED BOOK ONE

DERIVED

CAREY DECEVITO

DEDICATION

To Nick, Isabella, Addison & Kim

ACKNOWLEDGMENTS

I owe a debt of gratitude to my husband and two girls. Suffice to say, I wouldn't be where I am at this very moment without your never-ending support, sacrifice and encouragement.

Clarise (CT Cover Creations), your talent blows me away. Thank you for your support, encouragement and excitement for each and every one of our projects no matter how big or small.

Karen, my editor extraordinaire, your dedication to your craft has me in stitches at times when you manage to spot what others haven't. I look forward to more laughs, more work, and a friendship that transcends time.

Joanne, my proofreader and consort. Word will never express how much I appreciate your keen eye and friendship. I look forward to many more coffee dates where we plot out the fate of our characters. Now hurry up and let the world see how great I think you are.

To my betas. Your excitement and devotion to see me put out the best of my best has me always looking forward to working with each and every one of you. I love you all to pieces. Thank you for being my seekers of quality.

And last, but certainly not least, to my readers. Enough can't be said about how much I appreciate your love for words. It's what brings us together, and sure hope that you enjoy Payton's journey.

PROLOGUE

There are many things about this world that can't be explained; I, for one, and how I came to be. I'm not talking about how my folks met, the fact they fell in love, or the part about the birds and the bees. Let's face it; I need that mental picture about as much as I need a hole in my head.

Like I said, there are things in this world that are inexplicable. Some are dark, some are haunting, and others are wonderful, perhaps even seen as a gift. *Magical,* if you will. I tend to fall in one of those categories. Which one at this point, I'm not quite sure of; everything is still so new to me.

For as long as I can remember, I've led a sheltered life. From a young age, I was taught beauty existed in many different facets. Some possessed it externally, others were blessed with it on the inside, some with a combination of both, and then you had those unfortunate souls who possessed neither. My parents did their best to shield me from the latter.

I'd been told numerous times—too many to count really—I was special. It was something I'd always chalked up to what all parents tell their kids. Don't get me wrong, by the age of fifteen I knew I wasn't like everyone else. Feeling a humming sensation at your fingertips, whenever you touch someone, pretty much goes a long way to solidifying that perception. Call it instinct, inkling, or perhaps even a conviction based on the above; I knew I was destined for something bigger than the life that was splayed before me. For one, I seemed to be incredibly attuned with everyone's emotions, so much so, I found myself overwhelmed by them. My parents further confirmed my newly discovered abilities when I'd come home crying about an incident at school—one that seems so petty now—but I needed to know the truth. If only they'd warned me to brace for what would happen next; causing my world to tilt on its axis, forever changed.

This is my story—my rendition—of how I came to be…

CHAPTER 1

THE WATCHER

She threw one last assessing gaze into the hallway mirror, smiling back at herself.

Her all-black outfit hugged her curves in just the right places.

Fuck, this is torture. Why'd I have to be chosen for this?

Her makeup wasn't overly done, but those luscious red lips of hers were painted as though she aimed to sin tonight.

That hair. How I'd love to run my fingers through it, see if it were as soft as it looked. Long, lustrous, and black. The silkiest. I found myself imagining how it would feel as it draped down over her shoulders, tickling the skin of my chest, over my stomach…

Fuck, you must think me some kind of creep, don't you?

But I'm not.

I was chosen to be here.

For her.

For Payton.

Lives depended on it, and hers was the most important.

So I'd do my duty, then get the hell out of Dodge, because Black Beauty was simply just too much of a temptation.

Following my mark on the back of my Ducati Diavel, I pulled over a block away as her taxi came to a stop in front of the only bar on that street: Slick's.

This place wasn't one I'd seen her go to in quite some time. In fact, all she seemed to do was work, study, and sleep.

From my own research, I knew money had become tight since her parents' deaths nearly a year ago. She took courses for a Public Relations degree—I had no idea what she planned to do with it afterward—and she worked at one of my favorite haunts—Delicatessens—in the downtown core of Port Hope.

As her watcher, I've noticed her losing weight and looking increasingly stressed and tired over the last few months. I knew her situation would only get tougher, seeing as I'd overheard a phone conversation of hers mentioning she'd gotten herself a new job and wasn't planning on letting go of her other one. I sympathized with her plight.

When she'd entered Slick's, I waited a few, then followed her inside, recognizing a few people had already caught on to the magnetism she emitted and warding some of them off with a simple glower. Eyes can be convincing at times with their messages, sometimes more than one would imagine.

PAYTON

Tonight was going to be one of my last free nights of frivolity for a long while, which meant I was determined to make the most of it.

Approaching the bar, I'd expected for at least one of my girls to be waiting for me by now but found none.

Ordering a drink while I waited on them, I chose to enjoy the music, allowing the thrumming of the bass vibrating through my body to sway my hips to the beat.

"Well, if it isn't the birthday girl!"

A grin spread onto my face, and I turned to see my oldest and dearest friend, Sahara, standing there. An excited squeal escaped us both as we lunged at each other for one of those body-quaking hugs.

"Sweets, it's been too long." I smile at her, then ask, "Where are the others?" while looking around behind her for any sign of the rest of our crew.

"Washroom." Cue her signature eye-roll, which had me giggling.

"Things haven't changed, I see."

Part of that fact relieved me. When the girls had left for university, leaving me to fend for myself, I'd been afraid everything would change. In some cases, some things have. We've all grown older for one; but despite the distance that now separated us more often than not, we'd remained close, probably in thanks to our weekly group Skype chats.

So back to the rest of my kickass gang of girls…

Bethany and Brittany Callem are known in our small circle as the devil twins. Although twins by birth, it's their high-maintenance personalities and their ability to draw trouble their way, in almost any setting, that gained them their moniker. Their hearts were the biggest out of anyone I knew however, and that made them the best of the best in my book.

As for Sahara Jones, she and I have known each other relatively our entire lives. Both of us, including the twins, have been inseparable since middle school when Johnny Jones had tried two-timing Bethany and myself in the schoolyard. We were incredibly young, but sharing your cupcake with someone, then changing your mind about it the next day to share it with someone else was serious shit back then. Needless to say, Sahara and Brittany joined forces and gave poor Johnny something to think about with a few slaps and a kick somewhere, which perhaps was a little too much. With the way he went crying to the nearest teacher and the stern talking-to we all got from our parents, not to mention the school principal, I kind of felt bad for the kid. Sort of. I mean, he did take back his cupcake promise after all.

I may have other friends, but those three were the only ones I couldn't do without.

When Mom and Dad passed, the three of them were there to help me pick up the pieces. I was devastated, albeit also proud of us when the day came for all of us to go our separate ways.

Now—this weekend to be exact—marked a major milestone in my life. Tomorrow would be a year since my parents had been brutally murdered in front of me, leaving me alone—a story you'll come to understand fairly soon I'm afraid.

Two bodies latched on to either side of me, knocking me back from my reverie as a singsonged, "Happy Birthday!" rattled my ears.

I giggled. "It's not my birthday, yet," then rushed them both for a hug.

"A technicality! It will be at the stroke of twelve," Brit said, stepping back, taking me in and fanning her face with her hand dramatically. "Love the outfit."

"This old stuff?" I smirked, posing to gesture to my black, metallic V-neck halter, black skinny jeans, and my high-heeled boots.

"You're gonna slay some guy tonight with that outfit," Beth agreed.

Truth be told, I'd only been on a handful of dates, most of them never fully measuring up. All but one: Gage Wright. Gage had been a total sweetheart, or so I thought.

Somewhere between my parents' deaths, my healing, and life changing, Gage's and my relationship was left out in the cold. I still ached to feel his presence from time to time, but you know how life goes. It could be quite unfriendly at the worst of times. It twisted, turned, and bent you out of shape, only to do it over and over again. And even though you hadn't managed to straighten yourself out just yet, it took your legs right from under you for another tumultuous round. That's what changed us, and ultimately, it led to our relationship's demise. He left Port Hope and never looked back. It's safe to say, I never thought of looking back either, nor do I ever plan on it. There wasn't any hope, not after what he did to me.

THE WATCHER

Overhearing Payton talk about her experience with her ex had me thinking back on that night in particular.

My blood boiled at the recollection.

I'd just begun my duties that night, as a matter-of-fact.

She'd gone over to the dirtbag's house with a grocery sack, which looked as if it was about to blow its contents all over the walkway to the home. She looked like a woman on a mission.

Bending over, she retrieved what I realized was a key, which she set into the tumbler, turned, then let herself in.

Within moments all hell broke loose.

"What the fuck is going on?" I heard her scream.

"Uh. Hi?" some other woman said.

What the hell?

"Out!" my mark yelled, fury clearly making itself heard. "You!" I could hear something thump to what I could only presume being the floor.

Next thing I knew, I heard an, "I'll call you," and I managed to rush from the edge of the front door to hide at the side of the house, as some naked chick came flying out.

As soon as Naked Girl disappeared, Payton came flying out in a rage.

"Babe," the jackass began, as he tried to do up his jeans, but she'd hushed him by holding her hand up. "I can explain."

"You can explain?" she asked him bitterly. "Maybe you can explain why you're not at school right now? Maybe you can explain who that bitch is? Maybe you can explain to me why I've wasted a year of my life with someone like you?" Her hand met her forehead in a gesture of disbelief. "I can't believe I was about to give you what you've been asking for."

"Pay–"

"Never mind," she said. "I don't want to hear it. I thought we had something special. Clearly, we don't. I thought you loved me. Boy, was that a lie!" Huffing, she took a deep breath. I could tell she was fighting tears of betrayal, and I simply wanted to walk up to her, introduce myself, and make things better.

Yeah, I had it bad almost instantly.

"I do love you, Payton," the idiot had the audacity of saying.

"Tell that to someone who cares, because as of right now, I don't," was her rebuttal. "Goodbye, Gage." Turning to leave, she was one foot down the front step when he grabbed her wrist, pulling her back into him.

It took everything I had not to go up to him and make the guy eat my fist.

"I can't let you leave like this," he said, almost at a whisper.

"But I have to," she told him, never meeting his gaze.

"You were never mine." That's when she finally turned and walked out of his life—never to return.

PAYTON

"Earth to Payton!" Sahara giggled, as she waved a drink in my face.

I gladly took it from her hand, needing its assistance to rid me of the memories that had just flashed through my mind, what with having to explain why entertaining a relationship wasn't really on my radar.

"Thanks," I mumbled with a slight smile, taking a large sip.

"Where'd you go off to?" she asked me with Beth and Brit standing there, checking out the scene.

"Nowhere," I told her. I clinked her glass to mine and smiled, this time the gesture being easier to muster. "Cheers to us, ladies!" I cheered and chugged the rest, setting the glass down. Then I chased that drink with the shot the twins had ordered me, while I explained why I wasn't into going home with anyone tonight.

We hung out by the bar, talking for a while before we realized the liquor had been pooling in our systems, rendering us rather tipsy when we finally got up to our feet. Choosing to dance it off, we headed for the dance floor. On our way there, I felt a hand roughly palm my ass. Pissed off at the audacity of the male, I turned to pull his hand off me.

"Do you mind?" I snapped, and grabbed his package hard through his jeans, and gave him a stern look as his eyes bulged in shock. "I suggest you keep your paws off before I rip your jewels to shreds." I let go abruptly and turned to find myself facing three wide-eyed girls. They all had a look of surprise strewn across their faces. Suffice to say they had never seen this side of me before—this was new—something I'd developed having to go at it alone.

"Well, I expect that we know who can take care of herself now." Sahara's laugh came with a slight nervous undertone.

"Fucking bastard!" I muttered under my breath.

"You're hot, of course they want a piece of you," Brittany interjected.

"I'm not a damn steak," I told them, chuckling at my lame analogy. "Besides, I already told you guys, I'm not interested in anything with anyone right…" My voice trailed off as my gaze made contact with the brightest blue eyes I had ever seen. Smiling back shyly at the owner of those baby blues, I felt myself physically being pulled in the opposite direction by the girls, causing me to break the contact I had with him.

Why did he seem so familiar?

CHAPTER 2

THE WATCHER

A few hours later, she'd made her way home, sharing a cab with her girlfriends. One of them—Sahara, I think—had offered to stay the night, but she'd waved her offer away, telling her she'd better come and visit tomorrow before she took off.

Seated on my motorcycle, I watched as lights on the main floor went from on to off, a singular room upstairs being the only one left illuminated.

I pictured the raven-haired beauty getting ready for bed. Did she wear pajamas or go commando? Was she into satin and lace or favor cotton? Was she thinking about that one moment where our eyes connected earlier, because I sure as hell couldn't get the interaction off my mind.

I knew I was in trouble. I'd gotten too close.

But I can't help it.

When the lights turned off, I knew it was time to go. The morning would come all too soon and my duties would forever continue.

PAYTON

I woke to a loud thud in the room next to me. Wiping the sleep from my eyes, my senses being regained, a whimper came through from the other side of my bedroom wall.

I immediately sat up, wondering what could be going on. Something was telling me things weren't right.

Filled with dread, I got up, my feet feeling like they were touching ice. My bedroom felt foreign suddenly, and my heart sank as I felt a stabbing pain in my abdomen. Clutching my stomach, I knew this wasn't normal. I straightened myself up, the pain fading away, and proceeded to walk to my closed bedroom door. Quietly, my hand turned the knob and I exited my room, into the hall where I found my mother, lying on her stomach, arms stretched above her head as she attempted to crawl toward me.

"Payton, run, honey!" she yelled, blood sputtering from her lips. "It's time to run, sweetheart."

Sitting up abruptly, I wiped the sweat from my brow.

When will these nightmares end? I asked myself.

Maybe never.

I tossed.

I turned.

I threw pillows around.

When I finally gave up on sleep, I cursed my damn nightmares and the fact my alarm clock read 10:00 a.m. I was normally an early riser, one who felt as though I'd just wasted half of my day away by trying to make up on my lack of sleep.

It had been six months since I'd last had to relive my gruesome past in my subconscious. I thought I was done with those dreams.

Getting up, and despite feeling odd, I dressed in my workout clothes.

A good run would help.

Heading downstairs, I shoved my shoes on, grabbed my iPhone and earbuds, and headed to the front door, locking it, then shoving the key in the built-in pocket to my leggings.

Halfway through my run, I had reached Memorial Park when I began feeling even more off, for the lack of a better description. My stomach was beginning to churn, knots felt like they were forming within it, and my head began to pound. I shook it off and tried to pace myself for the second half of my run.

Five minutes from my house, my knees buckled due to the piercing pain in my temples. Sitting on my knees, on someone's front lawn, I attempted to breathe through the overwhelming throbbing pain while clutching at my head.

THE WATCHER

It wasn't until halfway through her run, when she'd reached Memorial Park that I noticed something seemed to be up with my charge.

The moment Payton collapsed—not even two blocks from her home—clutching her head and looking like she was in excruciating pain, did I start reevaluating my mission.

Part of me wanted to rush straight to her, but I'd already been so close—too close at that.

The other part of me—the professional one—felt as though I had a job to do, and my sense of devotion to duty was a value that had been instilled in me since birth. I was doing this for the sake of my family, for friends…for my kind.

Without realizing it, my feet began moving forward in the woman's direction, coming to a stop close enough to be seen in her field of vision.

My hand reached for her shoulder—heat seared through the simple touch—freaking the shit out of me.

Yeah, I was in trouble all right, and worst of all, I had to start this quasi-relationship based on a lie. I sure hoped my acting was foolproof.

PAYTON

A pair of shoes in sight.

A heated touch.

When did I get so cold?

"Hey! Are you all right?" a soft-spoken manly voice asked.

"I'll be fine," I told my concerned bystander, my head still hanging in my hands.

I tried to pick myself up, only to collapse back down to the ground, my vision beginning to blur slightly.

"I'm taking you home," he said, as he crouched down to my level, making a grab for my elbows in an attempt to aid me to my feet.

"No, honestly I…" My voice trailed off when I found myself looking upward into familiar eyes. "It's you," I said with a slight air of surprise.

"Huh?"

He helped me to my feet slowly. This stranger intrigued me so much; there was no way I was running home yet, that's for sure. The pounding in my head eased off, but the churning in my stomach continued, its knots growing progressively tighter, the unsettling getting worse.

"You're that girl," he said.

That was when I realized it was the guy from the club the night before—Mr. Bright-Eyes.

"That girl?" I eyed him, curious as to what he meant by it.

"I saw what you did to that dude after he grabbed you. It looked like you instilled the fear of God in him with whatever you told him," he said. "Then again, grab any guy by the balls like that, and I'm sure he wouldn't dare mess with you any time soon."

He chuckled, clearly noticing the heated blush that spread across my face.

"You saw that, huh?" I couldn't look at him, and I suddenly felt like I should keep making my way home. So I began to walk away.

"Where are you going?" He took the two quick steps to fall in stride beside me. My legs were strong, but the jelly feeling was getting stronger and stronger within them. The last thing I needed was another collapse. Especially in front of a handsome stranger.

"Home," I answer.

"Let me walk you."

Despite my half-hearted protest, I caved and felt an immediate sense of relief. I could feel the earlier symptoms slowly creeping up on me once again as he escorted me home. Reaching my front walkway, he almost seemed disappointed we had arrived at my house. I knew I wasn't going to be hearing the end of it after I noticed Sahara's car parked on the side of the street.

"Where the…" Sahara said, jumping out of her car. "Damn, Payton, are you all right?"

"I'm fine," I told her as everything started to blur. I felt Mr. Bright-Eyes' hand on my elbow, as I tried to brace myself. My ears began to ring while my eyes eventually registered black. The last thing I remembered was being lifted into strong arms, as though I weighed next to nothing.

Quietly, my hand turned the knob and I exited my room into the hall, where I found my mother lying on her stomach, arms stretched above her head as she attempted to crawl toward me.

"Payton, run, honey!" she yelled, blood sputtering from her lips. "It's time to run, sweetheart." My head registered panic but my body was unable to follow my mother's orders. A man flew out of the entryway to my parents' bedroom with my father pressed to his front. I didn't notice the knife sticking out of him until he started to slouch down, life draining from his body. Black eyes, deep as the deepest of abysses stared back at me. They appeared as though they were trying to swallow me whole. I felt the instant my father's soul left his body. My mother was lying limp at my feet, her own blood gurgling in her throat, with what I'd resolved myself to believing were her last breaths. I shuddered at the thought of what my fate held for me. The hunter took a step toward me. Fear settled deep inside.

"Come here," he ordered. My feet found their path as I started to back away from him. "I said, come here!" he ordered again, this time at a yell.

That was when I spun around to make my way downstairs, only to find myself hitting a brick wall; or so I thought. Hands gripped me at the wrists, while the hunter who had killed my father marched toward me.

There are two of them?

They were identical in appearance. One with deep black eyes, the one who killed my father and left my mother for dead; the second, with brown eyes and flecks of black in them. Regardless of color, they were the eyes of killers—they, the hunters—and I, their prey.

"What do you want?" I asked, fear lacing every shaky word that rolled off my tongue.

"You." And I felt something hard, hit me at the back of the head.

I woke up in a pool of my mother's blood mixing with mine. A heavy weight on my chest; those same dark black pools for eyes, merely inches from mine. I couldn't help but wonder what he was trying to do. His mouth moved closer to mine, but our lips never touched. My body ached from the abuse they had inflicted on it while I had been unconscious. The tensed air with frustration filled my senses. I could tell that whatever they were looking for, they hadn't found. I became consumed with feelings of anger and rage.

"Billy, I don't think…" His voice trailed off in frustration.

"Never mind that. Here." I saw the shiny blade being passed to him, but Billy shook his head. "Finish her off. She's no good to us anyway."

"I want to feel her life drain away." He looked at me with the evilest smirk.

Next thing I knew, everything faded and became black as Billy wrapped his roughly calloused hands around my neck, attempting to drain the remainder of my life out of me. In that moment, I let the darkness take me, hoping it would whisk me away, sparing me from feeling the painful doom my parents had succumbed to.

"Payton!" I felt light taps on the side of my cheek. "Come on, Payton, you have to wake up."

"Hmm," I mumbled groggily.

Sahara?

"That's it, Payton. Open those emerald eyes for me, hon," I heard.

Slowly coming to, more of my senses returning, I was increasingly aware of what had just happened. Bolting upright, I found myself sitting on my couch, Sahara crouched on the floor beside me.

"What the hell just happened?" I whispered out loud.

"You looked deathly ill and then you just passed out," she explained.

"Where's Mr. Bright-Eyes?" I asked her, looking around. There was no way she would have been able to get me in my house without his help.

"He's gone now. Where'd you find him?" she asked me.

"The club last night," I whispered, too many thoughts running through my head.

"I was with you last night, hon. You weren't with anyone."

"I mean I saw him there last night," I told her.

"But that doesn't explain him being with you today," Sahara persisted.

"I don't know. I had this pounding ache in my head and my knees gave out; he popped out from the middle of nowhere," I told her. "It doesn't matter. I'm fine now." I got up and headed to the kitchen for a glass of water. Truthfully, I was freaked out by what had just happened. The nightmare during my loss of consciousness shook me some.

"You're fine?" Sahara got up and chased me down. "Is that all you're going to say? For crying out loud, you scared the shit out of me, woman!" she practically yelled at me.

"I'm sorry?" I turned to face her, with an innocent smirk on my face, after I had poured myself a drink. "I hope he wasn't too freaked out," I said, in an attempt at diffusing her worry for me.

"He was worried, like I am now." Sahara studied me. "How long have they been back?" she asked, regarding my newly returned nightmares.

"Last night and just now have been the first," I admitted.

"It's been a year," Sahara thought aloud more than stating.

I nodded gloomily. "Yeah."

We spent a few hours talking about what we had missed out in each other's lives over the past year, since she had left for college—a welcome change of topic. I pretty much listened, seeing as nothing extensive had taken place with me other than work, my breakup with Gage—which she already knew about—and school, which again, she already knew this too due to our numerous Skype conversations.

"Are you sure you'll be all right while I'm gone?" she asked.

"I'll be fine," I assured her. "Go have fun with the family. Tell your parents I say hi."

"Will do and happy twenty-first birthday, sweets."

With that, my lifelong best friend took off. I stood in the doorway, watching as her car headed down the road, unable to shake the feeling that something in the air gave off a twinge of eeriness. I felt watched. Trying to rid the thought from my head, I closed the door, bolted it, then headed upstairs for a well-deserved shower.

CHAPTER 3

PAYTON

I was lathering my body with lotion when I noticed it. There, on my hip, I found a very faint but still very distinctive marking—in the form of a script-like spiraled circle— joining one that had appeared in my teens. I had no clue what those markings meant; only that they always seemed familiar somehow, and I loved them. My mother had similar ones, only they had been on the small of her back. A conversation with my parents, from what seemed like ages ago, came to mind. I'd been about fifteen at the time.

"Honey, please come and sit," my mother told me, gesturing to the dining room chair at the head of the table, while my parents proceeded to sit on either side of me. I had come home in an emotional fit, which had hit me from nowhere.

"Your mother and I have been meaning to talk to you about something. I didn't think it would be this soon, but it's obviously necessary," my father added.

"What is it?"

"Payton, what happened today," he began, "was something you'll come in time to understand and control."

"Your father's right, sweetheart."

"These feelings you're being bombarded with, they aren't necessarily your own," he proceeded.

"I know that, Dad. Today wasn't the first time," I confessed, as I watched my parents for their individual reactions; a look shared that only told me this wasn't going to be a short conversation.

I had learned more about my empathic abilities—along with various ways to channel and ignore them when need be—how to put up a wall, per se. It was only under times of stress when I actually lost some control and wasn't able to always block the flood of emotions that would come barreling toward me. What scared me the most out of that long discussion was my parents' second revelation. Now, you'd think being an empath, I would bask in the glory and be comforted by the fact I was able to tell what various people were feeling, but no. No matter how many times my parents stressed to me I should view my gift as a blessing, I saw it more as a curse. I couldn't just be normal, or just an empath; I had to be some kind of hybrid—a monster of sorts—a freak. Something out of a Greek mythology book. At the age of fifteen, you can only imagine my delight at finding out I was going to become some kind of soul-sucking, sexual dynamo of a character. No wonder my parents secluded me all these years! The good thing—I had until my twenty-first birthday before that part of me became active.

"So it begins," I whispered to myself, as I stared at my naked body in the bathroom mirror. Aside from the events from this morning's run, and this newly acquired body art of mine, I felt normal.

Yeah, as normal as you can be, despite what you are.

THE WATCHER

I could tell she was restless.

I'd watched as she attempted to settle in with some schoolwork. That had lasted about forty-five minutes or so.

Then she'd moved on to the TV, channel surfing. I tell you, it's a miracle she hadn't worn off the buttons.

At some point, she'd paced the house, peeking through the curtains a time or two, peering at the surrounding neighborhood, then the sky.

I'd been here since the sun rose this morning, following her on her run, saving her when she'd needed it, but once I'd seen she was safe with her friend, it hadn't taken me long to bail.

Part of me wondered if this woman even knew how powerful she was.

Payton's magnetism had been a force so strong; even I had a hard time breaking its pull, especially after we'd physically made contact. Something inside of me called to her, to keep her safe, to make her mine.

But you can't. Those weren't your orders.

By the third time she peered through her curtains—that look of suspicion strewn across her face—I knew her senses were as heightened, as mine were.

Something felt off—yet everything looked as normal as could be—nothing out of place.

PAYTON

The sky had started to cloud over, making the world around me look somewhat ominous, despite everything being as it should. It was the phone ringing that broke me from my thoughts of doom and gloom.

"Payton Lilith Mayfair-Devonshire, your head is playing tricks on you again," I told myself aloud as I headed to the coffee table to pick up.

The twins wanted to take me out again tonight. Despite the fact that it was Sunday, the urge to kick back no longer seemed as appealing as it once was. I figured I'd head out for a night on the town with the ladies, minus Sahara, who was now gone on a family holiday. Maybe this restless feeling would subside if I got out.

Changing into a dark violet strapless dress, which I always thought made my eyes pop—something I felt I needed today of all days to make me feel better about myself and the changes coming—I headed out to a late dinner with my friends.

"Who are we dressing for tonight?" Bethany asked me, as I jumped into the back seat of her car.

I smirked. "I'll take that as a compliment," I said, as she turned and shifted the car into drive, idling away from the curb.

If I'd only known how weird the night before me would become…

As we sat there eating and chatting, it didn't take me long to find myself being eyed by relatively every person in the restaurant—men and women alike. Our server had spent a considerable amount of time devouring me with his eyes as he took our respective orders, his gaze not once leaving me, even as he spoke to the twins. It made me feel like a total piece of meat, served up to perfection for everyone around me. It was disconcerting, yet despite disliking the attention, a part of me—that I equated to the succubus part—seemed to like, even thrive on it.

"Did you see how he looked at her?" Brittany asked her sister, once the server had finally left our table.

"Everyone's eyes are on you, Pay," Beth stated, with a nod in response to her sister, emphasizing her words by pointing a thumb over her shoulder.

I blushed, wishing I could simply melt into the wall behind me. I was never good with receiving an absurd amount of attention. Something apparently, I'd have to get used to.

A sense of relief washed over me the moment we stepped foot out of the restaurant. When the girls had mentioned they wanted to head to Slick's, however, it took them a considerable amount of time to convince me until I hesitantly agreed. After all, we were dressed to the nines with nowhere to go, and none of us wanted to end the evening so early. It was better than my other option, which was to go home and sit on the couch, bored out of my mind.

After a few hours of dancing, I pulled myself away to head to the ladies' room.

Eyes followed me, yet again. I can't explain the feeling straight up, but as eerie as it felt, I couldn't help the surge of excitement that pulsed through me. Despite this newfound sensation however, I shrugged it off, choosing to blame it on the liquor.

On another note, my ever so permanent empathic wall kept crumbling down around me, only for me to have to force it back up again. It was frustrating, and I blamed my new succubus mojo on that one.

Maybe I should have stayed home, the thought occurred as I'd reached the bathroom door, yet as quick as I was to think that, something inside of me felt repulsed at the idea.

After a quick stop in a stall and a handwashing, I had managed to cool myself down from the projected emotions of those unnamed faces out in the crowd. Weaving through the masses, overwhelming lust radiated toward me. A thirst so potent overcame me, heating my core. This one I knew had nothing to do with the alcohol I'd ingested. It was of something more primal—sexual in nature—to be more precise. Something I hadn't felt since Gage and I had been together, and it had never been potent to that degree. It was entirely unnatural, and somewhat unsettling to say the least, seeing as I had no clue as to where these urges were coming from; although, I had my suspicions.

Reaching my girls, which were where I had left them: on the dance floor, I laughed. They were bumping and grinding with two very appealing men.

The sight had me licking my lips and lust clouding my mind.

What the hell is wrong with me?

Instead of joining them—and adding fuel to the fire raging inside of me—I headed toward the bar for a drink; this time water.

"It should be illegal to look this good," I heard in my ear, feeling breath fanning down the side of my neck and over my shoulder.

My pulse quickened, but I chose to ignore the guy with the cheesy pickup line. Grabbing my bottle of water, I popped the top off and took a quick drink before turning to find the owner to those ridiculously spoken words blocking my way. Under any other circumstance, this invasion of my personal space would have been deemed too close for comfort, but somehow I wasn't fazed one bit by his forwardness.

Seeing as this tall dark drink of a man wanted my attention, I figured I'd join the girls and have a bit more fun before calling it a night. I grabbed his wrist and pulled him toward the twins, who were still with their guys. Bethany gave me a wink and a nod of approval on my selection as

I let him dance up close behind me, giggling at my sudden lack of inhibition.

I was unsure what came over me. One minute, I was rubbing my backside on this guy's crotch, and the next, I had him pushed in the back corner, away from everyone, my lips fused to his as his hands traveled eagerly over my ass, pulling me further into him. It wasn't until his body began to go limp on me that I pulled away, noticing his eyes slightly beginning to bulge out of his head, the veins darkening around them, his nose, and lips. My hands dropped to my sides as I stepped back, looking at his skin's ghostly coloring. That's when I chose to run and darted off in full-fledged panic. I didn't care about the girls; they had their car and I could formulate some cockamamie story to satisfy their curiosity later. I had to get home—right the fuck now!

Fifteen minutes later, I jumped out of the cab, only to find myself looking at a dark house filled with awful memories from a year gone by. The only thing out of place about tonight was the visitor who sat on my front porch…

THE WATCHER

What a clusterfuck of a night.

My patience was wearing thin, and the rage I felt simmering inside of me was growing to the point I felt as though I was ready to burst.

She was my temptation—and I her salvation in this fucked up world—and I was ready to crack some skulls. It didn't matter if they were male or female; human or not at this point.

Why did she have to tease me so?

The moment her lips touched that sleazeball's, my feet

started in their direction. She had no ties to me, nor me to her beyond watcher and charge, but it felt so wrong—a stab to my gut.

Before I could reach Payton, however, I took notice of the blue veins spreading over the guy's face and neck, the strength leaving his grip on her fine ass, Payton pulling away with a face covered in an expression of horror.

Without noticing me, she barreled out of bar and straight into a cab, but not before I saw the tears streaming down her cheeks—and I was hot on her heels.

CHAPTER 4

PAYTON

I wiped away the silent tears that had continued to fall during my cab ride as I faced my visitor, forcing a smile.

"What are you doing here?" I asked him.

He stood up to greet me; a look of concern on his face. "I had to check up on you," he said, meaning he remembered what day it was.

Gage—my ex—stood there, looking as ruggedly handsome as he always had been. That hadn't been our problem, but it definitely had been our demise.

"How long have you been here?"

"An hour or so," he sheepishly answered, shrugging his shoulders, then rubbed the back of his neck. "Judging by the outfit, you're doing just fine." Was that a disgruntled tone I detected? It certainly didn't take an empath to know the man before me was riddled with nerves.

Why do I make him nervous?

He had always been cool, calm, and collected. Even when I focused on his emotions, he'd been that way. It had been nice and calming for me; but this version of Gage was different. I wasn't sure if I liked it, despite feeling victorious at the fact I suddenly had a nervous effect on him. I suppose he must have thought I wouldn't want to give him the time of day, which he was right about, but part of me felt like we'd never fully closed the door to our past. I hadn't wanted it, but tonight—of all nights—I needed answers.

Call me crazy, tired, or delusional, but I invited Gage inside. I was unsure as to the true nature of his visit, and honestly, I couldn't care less. The only thing I knew was, I didn't want to be alone right then and needed someone familiar around me. Gage was the lucky subject of my relief on that night, and I was going to finally put this chapter of my life to a close.

"I miss you," Gage told me, as we sat down on opposite ends of the couch, effectively bringing an end to our awkward silence.

Too close.

I got up and moved toward the mantle, grazing my fingers over the picture frames that held photographs of me and my family. I missed them so much, it was almost unbearable. When I didn't answer, I heard Gage clearing his throat.

"What?" I turned toward him.

"Well, I wasn't expecting silence," he said with a short tone.

"What did you expect? That after six months I'd run back into your arms?" I snapped. "The truth is, Gage, I am glad to see you. It only solidifies my sentiment that all you are good for is a piece of ass." Gage's face flushed with frustration. I knew he hadn't expected me to have answered him in that fashion. I was no longer the weak, demure woman he once took advantage of with his cheating ways. I was able to stand on my own two feet now—for that—I was thankful he had come into my life.

"Wow," he chuckled. "I'm kind of liking this outspoken version of you." Getting to his feet, he took a few steps toward me. I lifted my hand to signal for him to stop, but he continued, a cocky demeanor present in his body language. My defenses were wavering, and I could literally sense his lust seeping into my very core.

Fuck, not now.

The last thing I needed was a repeat from earlier tonight. Until I had some answers on what exactly this whole glitch of mine entailed, and how to control it, I couldn't risk it.

"Stop," I said, my voice cracking and sounding husky, but he closed the gap between us until the fronts of our bodies were slightly grazing.

"I can't," he whispered onto the skin that covered my collarbone, causing my pulse to quicken. My arms hung limp at my sides.

"You have to," I whispered, then cleared my throat. "We're not…" My voice left me altogether as I felt his soft warm mouth on the spot below my ear. A moan escaped my lips, but instead of feeling humiliated at giving in, the predominant emotion was a ravenous one. I wanted to devour him, get my answers, then make him go away.

After a few dozen seconds of battling the erratic thoughts inside my head, I deduced that giving in was my only option, seeing as my body was progressively betraying me. Despite all the obvious reasons why I should kick this sexy—nonetheless, a jerk—out of my house, whatever it was going on inside me simply had a greater hold over me; knocking all rational thoughts out of my head. My defenses were completely dysfunctional, therefore rendering me helpless and at Gage's mercy. It was very much trance-like.

Refusing to kiss him on the lips, I let him have his way with me. I don't even recall how we had gotten upstairs, let alone to my bed. I was too enthralled with the feeling of his body against mine, his hands playing me like the delicate instrument I was.

It was tonight that I had my first taste at sex—the oral

kind. Don't kid yourself, my virginity wasn't thrown out the window, discarded like an old toy I no longer needed, but I sure had managed to get a little closure. Oddly enough, I was glad it was with Gage—despite our history—I'd shared this new foray with; and not some one-nighter. But I would never give him my virginity. That was something I chose to do when it felt right, and that proverbial ship had sailed with the man. Still, it didn't mean I couldn't have my fun with him.

The flaming thirst, the same one that had formed within me at the club earlier tonight, finally had been somewhat quenched by his mouth between my legs, and mine sucking him dry. My body was invigorated, I felt alive, then I got up from the bed, leaving Gage lying there as I reached for my silk bathrobe.

"When did you get a tattoo?" he asked.

Freezing in my spot, I hadn't realized what I would answer if anyone would spot it.

"It was a gift to myself. I got it a few weeks ago," I lied.

He grinned, then said, "You sure have changed." His eyes clouded over with lust again before he patted the mattress at his side. "Come back to bed."

"I think you should leave," I told him in an out-of-the-blue fashion.

"What?" He sat up, the sheets dropping away from his upper torso, barely covering his package. I eyed him feeling hungry but knowing another taste of him would be entirely wrong for obvious reasons. And those answers I was seeking earlier? Yeah, I no longer felt the need for them.

"You heard me," I said, grabbing his pants and chucking them at him. "I have work tomorrow and you'll only keep me up with your snoring," I stated dismissively, which prompted him to get up and do as I had requested.

I woke up, feeling like a new woman. My muscles ached

slightly from last night's ventures with Gage, but my body was still riding its blissful high. I reminded myself that I should check in with Carly. She was my mother's baby sister—and a succubus at that. Surely, she'd know a bit about my situation. Mom had told me all the women in the family had what I'd dubbed as the 'mutant' gene. She was the only relative I had bothered to stay in touch with; all the others being deceased, dying, or dead to us due to an old family feud. Carly was more like an older sister to me than an aunt.

I'll give her a call after this shift, I told myself. That should keep her from hunting my ass down, seeing as I had yet to return her call from a few days ago, questioning me on anything new going on in my life. I knew what she wanted to know, and I realized I should have called her sooner, but I hadn't been ready to broach that conversation.

THE WATCHER

With my laptop in tow, I followed her for her shift at the bistro, which began at nine.

I was still fuming at the fact she'd let that good-for-nothing ex of hers in, when she'd gotten home the night before. The fact he came out in a pissed-off huff, buttoning his shirt, didn't make me feel better about what my mind had conjured on what must have happened between them.

Setting myself up to do some long-overdue work with a cup of coffee at my reach—I always made sure to stay out of her serving area—I proceeded to pull up the various documents I had to go over.

The day was pretty much normal until the lunch rush started. It seemed like the place was a magnet for men today, and every male eye in the place, coworkers included, was on Payton. I forced myself to stay seated—and had succeeded too—until one of her regulars decided to get fresh with her.

"So, Payton," he grabbed her wrist and pulled her back toward him. "What do I have to do to get you to give me five minutes of your time outside of this place?"

"It's easy. Nothing. I don't date customers," she told him, trying to pull her wrist out of his grip, only to have his hold on her remain intact. "Will you please let go?" She attempted to pull again, giving him one of her sweet smiles. I've seen guys try to pick her up before now, but nothing like this. I could sense that he was outright freaking her out. I could only imagine what was going through her head at a time like this, when her life was changing at a rapid pace.

"I don't think so." He got up from his chair, pulling her toward him so that they stood a foot away from one another at eye level.

No fucking way, buddy. Not on my watch.

Getting to my feet, I marched over so I stood right behind her. "Listen, jerk, the lady asked you to back off and let her go, so step off."

PAYTON

I didn't have to look to see who it was. It seemed as though I had inherited some kind of knight in shining armor. Turning, I found myself facing none other than Mr. Bright-Eyes himself.

I really need to find out his name. Mr. Bright-Eyes was bound to get old if we kept bumping into each other like these last few days.

"Bitch," the patron mumbled and turned to leave, kicking his chair so it tipped onto its back.

My hero walked around me and grabbed the chair to set it back on its legs.

Flustered, I asked, "What are you doing here?" My arms crossing over my chest, foot tapping as I awaited my answer.

His eyes gave me an approving once-over as he smirked. "Can't a guy just come in and eat?" The amused look twinkling in his eyes intrigued me. His teasing demeanor had me giving him a genuine smile.

"Seriously?"

"Honestly?" he asked, and I nodded for him to continue. "I had no clue you worked here, but I'm glad I came in today of all days. Now I get to check up on you. How are you feeling?" Something seemed off with his initial statement, judging solely by the twitch in his cheek, since I seemed to be unable to read his emotions right then.

"I'm better. Thanks." I looked down shyly. "I should get back to work."

His relieved smile brightened his face and I was quickly regretting having to get back to my duties. "Sure," he said.

"Thanks for yesterday, by the way," I told him, heading toward the kitchen.

"Don't mention it," he called out at my back.

Heading home after what I can definitely call my weirdest shift yet, I was glad my workday was over. Checking my messages using my cell, I found a text from Gage and another from my aunt. I deleted Gage's message without reading it and immediately dialed Carly's number. My aunt had officially managed to make everything going on and her worry seem so urgent, all of a sudden.

Half an hour later, I was sitting at Carly's kitchen table, talking and enjoying some dinner.

She finally broke our contented shared silence. "Anything odd happen lately?" My eyes met hers as my fork fell freely to my plate and she smirked. "I see you've noticed some changes."

"That's the understatement of the century. I'm a goddamn succubus!" I exclaimed with a slight panicked tone. To be honest, I had hoped my parents had been wrong, but at the same time, I wished I knew more about how I would be affected by it all, once I did come into those abilities. It hadn't even occurred to me to try and read up on shit, since my parents had been big on letting me know Google didn't know all about our kind.

After a few hours, I had left Carly's house happy to know more about this whole new part of me. It turned out I had caught on to things quite quickly. Carly had explained her first experience with a man, after her urges had hit her. He hadn't been quite as fortunate as my guy at the club— hers having died on her. She literally managed to suck the life out of the poor soul. The only thing Carly couldn't help answer was why my empathic defenses weren't working right with this whole new succubus business. She only shared that she thought it might be from having too much to control on my own emotional front, therefore leaving me weakened from blocking others until I needed to read into someone. From that aspect of things, I knew I was solely on my own with figuring things out.

Nothing new there, right?

CHAPTER 5

PAYTON

Walking home, I couldn't shake the feeling I was being followed. This was something that had recently come to pass—hence my obsession with looking out my house windows—despite everything being locked tight. Hell, even my patio furniture as of late hadn't been enjoyed during school assignments.

Thinking about what Carly had told me about being a succubus, wondering if I'd ever find a happy balance like my parents had; if I'd ever have a sense of normalcy, I lost track of my surroundings and fell deep in thought.

What was normal anyway? I suppose it was what we made it be, right? Until that fateful night when my parents had been stripped from me, I had no concept it was actually truthful that there were people around out for our kind; you know, us freaks, if I could put it mildly.

I still didn't know how I managed to survive that night, lying in my mother's blood, but I somehow couldn't shake the words out of my father's mouth, six years ago when I had learned of my fate.

"There will be a time to run, and a time to fight," he told me.

"Why fight? Why run? What are you not telling me, Dad?" I asked him, slightly irritated at these convoluted riddles of theirs. My mother and father exchanged a worried look.

"Some people, some of our kind more specifically, are looking for more power over the humans," he explained. "We call them hunters. They find themselves going after those who have multiple 'gifts' because it's a kill-two-birds-with-one-stone approach. It's quicker, leads to less bloodshed, but they won't hesitate to kill anyone who gets in their way either."

"I get they're after power, but what do they expect to do with it, really?" I asked of them.

"You have to understand that this world is delicate in the way it's balanced. There is a purpose to each of our gifts. It may never be fully known from the beginning, and some are easier to tame and to accept than others," my father told me, and I knew he was referring to my empathic abilities compared to the ones I was to receive on the day of my twenty-first birthday.

"I don't see anything positive coming out of sucking someone's life force out of them," I'd mumbled with an air of resentment.

"You speak of it all as if it were a curse." My mother's eyes watered. I could tell she blamed herself.

"Isn't it, though?" My words were mixed with a certain degree of disdain.

"If you look at it that way, sweetheart, that's all you'll ever see," she told me, as she reached for my clasped hands that sat on the tabletop. "In the human world, you'd be regarded as a freak. In the Fae world, you represent all things youthful, loving, and beautiful. Our purpose is not always known from the beginning, but yours will come to you all in good time."

"But can't you tell me what it is?" I asked.

"We can't. To do so could alter the final outcome," my father explained.

"Outcome?" I asked puzzled. My father nodded as I studied his face, waiting for him to elaborate on that statement.

"Yes, the outcome. When the time comes, you'll know more; but until then, please don't push for answers you cannot yet fully understand, my baby girl," he said.

Steps quickened from behind me, effectively knocking me out of my reverie.

I was being followed; I just knew it!

I must have been ten minutes walking distance from my house. Despite my aching feet, something told me to run and see if I could lose this person. I had no inclination of looking back to see who my follower was. I put foot to pavement and raced like my life depended on it. I cut through an alley, and headed back the way I came, before cutting through a side street, and hiding behind a large bush in a neighbor's yard. When I figured I had waited long enough, I came out of my hiding spot and walked out; only to hear the quickening of those same steps behind me again.

Taking off like a bat out of hell, I sprinted away, only to turn a corner and crash into what felt like a brick wall, which I bounced off of and landed flat on my ass onto the sidewalk.

Two strong hands picked me up and set me back down on my feet as I tried to dart off, looking behind me, worried my follower would manage to succeed at catching up to me with whatever his or her purpose was.

Realizing I wasn't going anywhere fast, with this strong grip keeping me still, I began to twist to see if I could free myself, officially thinking that maybe I'd been captured.

"Let go!" I shouted, busy looking behind me, the feel of panic becoming too overwhelming.

"Calm down, Payton," I heard.

Snapping me out of my freak-fest, I collapsed into *him*. Almost immediately, I remembered my parents' heedful warning of these hunters never stopping until they got what they wanted. I scrambled out of his arms and yanked on his shirt, attempting to drag him along with me, but he didn't budge.

Why couldn't I be gifted with superhuman strength with all this bullshit? I thought to myself.

It definitely would have come in handy.

"We have to go, now!" I told him, but he held his ground. "I have to get away."

"Get away from whom? Payton, there's no one there." He grabbed my face between his hands and forced me to look at him.

Mr. Bright-Eyes' gaze held mine. I never expected it to be him, but somehow—the minute our eyes made contact—I calmed, my wits being regained.

"Can I let you go now?" he asked, still holding onto the sides of my face, his eyes not straying from mine.

"Yeah," I said, taking a deep breath. Could his eyes really be that blue? I mean, they were glowing like sapphires. Finally, able to pry my eyes from his, I smiled, slightly embarrassed from my fine display of lost control.

"Can I walk you home?" he offered.

"Sure," I answered, trying to make sense of his calming effect over me.

It turns out that Mr. Bright-Eyes has a name: Rafael Nottingham as it happens, or Rafe as he preferred. I spent our entire walk listening to him talk, learning more about him. It was more than he would ever know about me, but for our own good, I knew it had to be that way. He moved to the city a year ago, to help out his grandmother while he finished his last year of college. He fully admitted to having a quirky family, but he loved them despite those eccentricities. His words, not mine.

"I know they mean well, but sometimes, I swear, the stork dropped me off because I'm not like any of them," he finished.

"I'm sure you're more like them than you think," I said.

"Aside from physical similarities, you'd never know we were related," he stated with a light chuckle.

Before I knew it, we were standing at my front door, and I was toying with the idea of inviting him in.

A complete stranger.

One who'd been there for me far too often in the last twenty-four hours, to be honest.

"So I guess I owe you big time for sure now," I blurted out.

"It's nothing. Don't worry about it," he said.

"Says the guy who's always around to save my butt when I need rescuing," I teased him. "You truly have a hero complex, don't you?"

"Not really." He paused and studied my reaction. "I just happen to be there every time you fall."

That made me giggle. "Charmer."

"I try." He shrugged his shoulders, trying to portray a perfect picture of innocence, which made me laugh harder.

After a few more minutes of rather comical and enjoyable banter, Rafe decided to back away. I watched him leave as he turned and pretended to tip his hat to me in a gentlemanly gesture of farewell. I couldn't help the smile crossing my lips as I shut my front door and bolted it.

Moments later, I could no longer ignore what had happened earlier, prior to haphazardly running into Rafe. Picking up my cell, I dialed Carly's number, figuring it'd be best giving her fair warning as to my adventure after leaving her house. If someone had indeed followed me, they could very well be aware of Carly's whereabouts—not just mine.

After three tries, and my calls going to voicemail, I bit my bottom lip. Call me a worrywart, tell me it was my head playing games, or simply women's intuition, but something wasn't sitting right with me. For having left the woman with plans to unwind only half an hour prior, there was no reason for her not to pick up her phone.

Unless…

That all too familiar feeling of being watched I'd been having lately had returned…

CHAPTER 6

RAFE

In the following week, I had spotted a few known hunters in and around the places Payton would usually end up. The alley behind the bistro where she worked, her neighbor's yard, down the street from her place…the list goes on.

Needless to say, attention was very clearly drawn to her, and orders stated that I didn't make myself known until the time was right to those enemies.

What bothered me the most was my mark's one and only personal contact hadn't been in touch with me for far too many days as of yet. Despite my communicating this with my superiors though, there wasn't a thing I could do about it to help.

Only time would tell what would happen next.

PAYTON

Gage had called incessantly throughout most of the week. By the time Friday came around, I'd had enough of simply ignoring his calls and blocked him from my phone.

I was scheduled to start my bartending job tonight over at Slick's. That's right, the same club I love to let loose at—

coincidentally, the one where I'd nearly killed a man with a simple make out session—is the same club that occupies my weekend nights starting tonight.

Joe, the owner of the place, had requested I keep everything I wore for work to solid blacks and whites and avoided showing too much skin. Needless to say, it was an upscale establishment, and he prided himself as having classy looking workers, not slutty trash. Knowing I would be on my feet all night, I opted to wear my black leather knee-high boots, black skinny jeans with a white halter that hung loosely around the waist. I brought some extra sparkle to the outfit with some bangle bracelets, pendant earrings, and my makeup, which accentuated my green eyes. Opting to put my hair up for the night, I tied it up in a messy bun, which allowed for some loose tendrils to fall on either side of my face.

I walked into Slick's and headed to Joe's office, where the employees stored their belongings in the few lockers he kept there.

"How's it looking out there?" Joe asked me as I walked in.

I told him that the place was starting to fill up relatively quickly, and it was barely nine at this point.

Smiling at me, he said, "Good," and then looked down, typing away on his laptop and what looked like invoices.

Half an hour later, I was introduced to Holly, my partner behind the bar for the night. She was a tiny but extremely beautiful woman with a pixie looking haircut, and her small features were played up with dramatic looking makeup. There was no questioning why Joe had hired her, seeing as she had amazing skills behind the bar; especially when it came to bottle juggling. I swear, it was like something out of that Tom Cruise movie—please tell me you've seen *Cocktail*.

After a bit of small talk between customers, I

discovered I liked Holly; she was definitely someone I could see myself hanging out with from time to time, outside of work. She was spunky and despite her size, she knew how to handle her own with belligerent drunks, or so I had come to realize on a few occasions earlier this evening. Joe had come to help us out a little after eleven, when the crowd got larger than anticipated. It seemed like the live entertainment for the night had generated a substantially larger than usual influx of people who simply were looking for a good time, to put it mildly.

"Damn if Tina picked the wrong night to call in sick," he muttered in passing, as he caught his breath from a wave of mixing drinks that finally had dwindled in intensity.

"What'll it be?" I asked a group of self-assured men who had just walked up to the bar. I'm not sure if it was because of them, or if it was just me, but I was beginning to feel uncomfortable. Perhaps it was something they were projecting. I was sort of beginning to regret taking this job at this point. Being around a bunch of inebriated people, where the urges for sexual exploits were at their highest, might not have been ideal for a new succubus; one who had yet to fully control her urges and know everything she needed about her abilities.

"I'll take three Bud Lights and a piece of you on the side," one of the guys, most likely the leader of the group said, throwing a chuckle toward the male duo behind him as they stood there devouring me with their eyes. Despite the crawling feeling on my skin, my body began to feel heated. Channeling my empath side, I was able to tell that the leader of the trio wholeheartedly planned on acting out his fantasies with me, given the chance. Those thoughts excited me, yet petrified me to my core, all at the same time. I didn't understand why my body wanted to betray me when I was basically this guy's prey.

"Dream on," I chuckled, ducking down below and

reaching for the beer fridge, pulling out their three beverages. Popping the caps off each bottle, I handed them over and accepted his payment; his dollar-tip to my nineteen-dollar bill a complete insult to servers around the world. As I turned to head over to the register, his hand grabbed my wrist and held on. I turned to look at his hand on me, and then up to his eyes, with an expression that heeded warning his way.

Not this again.

"I suggest you let go of me now, before you regret it." The guy didn't budge. If anything, I felt his grip tighten as he pulled me toward him, leaning us over the counter of the bar. For once, I actually wished I could let myself lose control and give this guy exactly what he wanted, but most importantly, what he deserved. I can't believe I was contemplating draining him.

Maybe there is an upside to this whole succubus thing.

Joe came to my rescue and made sure the guys were escorted out of the club before anything serious could happen. He was very protective of his workers and I appreciated that from him.

Someone caught the corner of my eye as I turned to take care of a freshly washed load of glassware. Gage was there, and I couldn't help the feeling of annoyance that had just now overcome me.

"Joe, I'm taking five, if that's all right."

He nodded, seeing as I had refused to take him up on his break offers earlier. I had felt like it wasn't fair to leave them hanging and tending to the orders when it was so crazy busy.

I grabbed Gage and pulled him to the back of the bar, near Joe's office door, and cornered him.

"We need to talk," he said, quickly moving around me so I was forced to turn to face him, leaving me with my back against the wall. "I can't stop thinking about you."

"Gage, you need to go. I'm working," I told him, gulping as I felt him nuzzling my collarbone. If the circumstances were different, I might have entertained the idea of seeking sexual release from him, but it wasn't the time nor the place.

"I know you want this as much as I do," he whispered into the soft skin of my neck.

"Just because I want something doesn't mean I get it." I pushed him away. "Let's do this some other time. Please?" I gave him a slight pleading look.

"Fine. I'll wait for you to get off work. We can talk then," he answered in his classic pouting manner. Funny how I used to think it was cute, yet now, it grated on my last nerve.

"Do whatever you want," I mumbled my annoyance, and walked back to my post behind the bar, leaving him staring after me.

Gage sat at the bar in silence, even when Rafe came walking through the door. My savior and I spent some time making small talk and laughing between my serving customers. The band was phenomenal, and I felt myself wanting to stick around even after my shift ended. It seemed my body fed on the surge of emotions that floated in the air. You could literally choke on the lust, excitement, and envy that hung everywhere around us.

Returning from clocking out after my shift, I felt hands on my hips, pulling me backward; into that ever so popular corner I seem to be spending my off-time in lately.

"I'm taking you home, then we'll talk," Gage announced.

"No thanks," I answered. "I'm going to stick around, have a drink, maybe have a few dances, and go home on my own."

"Fine. I'll drive you home after you're done having your fun."

"Whatever," I said, as I walked away from him. "Joe, I'm going to need a shot of Jack," I called out to him, taking my place beside Rafe, leaving the poor man as a buffer between my ex and me.

"You want to dance?" Rafe asked, clearly reading the annoyance in my expression.

Smiling, I took his hand and let him lead the way, ignoring Gage completely.

I'm not sure if it was the shots I had taken, my empathic abilities, or any other outstanding factor that evaded me at that point, but my body was beginning to hum and feel heated. I hadn't spoken a word to my ex for nearly an hour. Annoyed at his childish shenanigans, I had chosen to ignore him, resulting in him giving Rafe and me death glares as we had fun dancing to the live music.

After a while of fuming on his barstool, Gage came up to us, and asked, "What are you doing?"

"I'm dancing, what's it look like?" I smirked as I swung my hips, slightly rubbing the front of my body against Rafe's.

"Are you ready to go home now?" he asked me on a yawn.

"No," I answered, then turned to look at a smirking Rafe quickly before returning my eyes back to my ex. "Go home, Gage. I'll talk to you tomorrow."

"I'm not leaving you here with this guy," he blurted out, so both Rafe and I had no problem hearing him over the music. If you asked me, it seemed like he was looking for a rise from Rafe; one he didn't get.

"Don't worry, man. I'll get her home safe." He winked at me. "I always have."

The look of fluster and confusion on Gage's face was

priceless. I was thankful he hadn't embarrassed himself further by causing a scene. I'm not sure how I would have dealt with that, and I was dreading the next conversation between us. He would definitely try to make me justify myself, not that I owed him any answers in the slightest.

I giggled. "So you know I'll have loads of explaining to do tomorrow, right?" I said, once Gage had gone through the bar's doors.

"Who is he anyway?" Rafe asked.

"My ex. He just came back into town and thought perhaps I had forgotten about his cheating ways," I explained.

"Now why would anyone in their right mind want to do that to you?" he asked the very question I had been wondering the answer to all this time.

"Can't you think of a reason at all?" I asked smartly.

"No." He paused, then groaned before he continued, "Look around you, almost every man in this place has been gawking at you. I don't see why he'd find someone else appealing if he already had you."

Well, how about someone who was willing to give it up to him when I didn't? But it wasn't the place for me to say anything about that.

"Well, well, Mr. Bright-Eyes," I teased him. "You're making me blush. Are you coming on to me?"

"I'm speaking the truth," he plainly said with a smirk. "And maybe just a little." I swear I felt him pulling me in closer, as I giggled once more at his statement.

I liked that he could get an honest laugh out of me. It felt good. There'd been too much sadness in my life in the last year.

An hour later, I was home, Rafe leaning on the edge of the doorway beside me as I unlocked my front door. I heard a car door slamming shut on the street, then all hell broke loose.

"So you're fucking him now?" I heard. Turning to face a raging Gage, I didn't know what to do with myself, my mouth dropping open, then slamming shut.

Rafe positioned himself between Gage and me.

Finding my words finally, I let loose. "What I do, and with whom, isn't of your concern," I told him from behind my savior.

"Bullshit!" Gage screams. "I told you I needed you back, and instead of talking to me, you find yourself a boy toy. How so very convenient for you, the cocktease who never gave it up."

"Get the hell out of here and don't come back!" I shouted.

"You heard her," Rafe spoke calmly.

"Mind your business," Gage growled at Rafe.

Then something odd happened. After a few silent seconds too long, and some weird stare down between the two guys, Gage pulled a one-eighty with his attitude.

"I'm s-sorry," he stuttered softly. "I'll leave you be."

Turning around, he left where he had come from. I hadn't expected that. In fact, I had expected the complete opposite; and so, I had braced myself for swinging fists and a few bruises between the two of them.

Clutching the back of Rafe's shirt tightly and pressing the side of my face into his back, I'd hoped the blowout I was expecting would never ensue. After Gage had driven off, Rafe finally turned around and pulled me away from him so he could look me over. What happened next, I never anticipated.

"I don't know how you do it, but I just can't take it anymore," he whispered against my lips, as his hands found my waist, and under my shirt. His fingertips played a delicate pattern on the tender skin located there.

"Why...How..." The words weren't coming out for me as I felt him nibble the soft skin below my ear, causing me to arch into him. "Oh…Never mind," I managed along with a low moan.

RAFE

The moment I got up close to Payton, her warm breath, fragrant with the beer and shots she'd drunk earlier at the bar, combined with the heat from her body, I was a goner.

I enjoyed saving her from her ex. I wouldn't have been opposed to kicking his ass if it meant having him leave us alone in the end, allowing me with more alone time with this complex vixen before me.

The scent of clear arousal had me inching even closer, nibbling the soft skin below her ear, causing her to arch into my chest.

Pulling back to gaze into those emerald eyes of hers, as if asking for permission, I saw the unfettered want and need there. So I did the next logical thing I could do.

I kissed her.

Hard.

Desperate.

I showed her how much simply being in her presence had me stuck on her.

The moment her mouth opened on a moan, I plunged my tongue in, getting the best taste I'd ever had from any woman I'd ever been with.

The way she clutched at my shoulders, bracing as though she needed me to carry her, to keep her safe, had me hard enough to hammer nails.

Easing back, I pecked her lips, then whispered, "I should go." Next I kissed the edge of her mouth. "Before I do anything we both regret in the morning." I kissed her forehead. "Goodnight, Payton."

Dumbstruck expression square on her face, I left her standing at her unlocked door, mouth swollen from my kisses, then turned to blow her a kiss once I'd reached the end of her walkway.

Tonight wasn't going to be the only time we'd kiss. That was a promise both she and I could take to the bank.

CHAPTER 7

PAYTON

Half an hour later, I was in bed—alone.

Rafe had respectfully pulled away as things began to get quite heated. Something made me want to simply let myself get lost in him, but not in the same way as with anyone else I'd ever dated. Not even Gage.

He was different.

Oh, but such a good different.

As I lay there in bed, thoughts of him being something other than human began to roam through my head. After all, how could I stand to kiss him on the mouth and it hadn't fazed him one bit? How do you approach a subject like that without outing yourself and inciting questions on his end? It's not like I could simply say, "Hey, by the way, how come you didn't suffocate to death while we made out last night?" or "By the way, I'm an empathic succubus, what are you?" Just when I thought I would be able to handle this new lifestyle of mine, Rafe changed the playing field all over again for me. Overwhelmed by all thoughts Rafe, I drifted off to sleep.

The following morning, I decided to give contacting Carly another try. She hadn't returned my calls all week long, and my continuing hypothesis something was amiss was only getting stronger. Instead of picking up the phone, I decided to head over to her house to see if I could find any trace of her. At least I'd be able to let myself in and make sure everything was as it should be.

After my inspection, nothing was out of place. The dishes were washed, her fridge was fully stocked, her bed was made as though someone was still there, yet everything seemed like it was left untouched somehow. I was pondering why my aunt would leave me high and dry, without a word, when I heard some movement above my head.

The attic?

Being ever so quiet, I found the release for the access hatch and slowly climbed up. I never expected to find Carly so easily, nor did I expect to find her in the state that she was in.

Deep into some kind of delirium, Carly was hunched, shaking in a cowering position in the far corner of the attic, storage boxes surrounding her.

"You can't have her!" she shouted, her voice not holding any power. Why was she so weak? How long had she been up there? These were all questions rolling about in my head, but I first had to get her in a semi-rational state to hear those answers.

"Have who, Carly?" I asked her softly.

"She's gone," Carly stated firmly.

"Gone where?"

The conversation went back and forth for the next few minutes, until I realized the 'she' Carly had been referring to was me.

"Carly, it's me." I attempted to crawl my way to her and stopped as she pushed herself further into her corner, seemingly wanting to melt into its walls. I hated myself for frightening her even more. "It's Payton."

"Payton?" she asked in a removed tone, as if she was in

some faraway world. Her body relaxed ever so slightly, but I could tell she was still petrified.

"That's right, Auntie Carly. It's me," I reassured her softly, and finally started seeing more obvious signs she was starting to lull even more; calming the internal panic that had struck her, who knows how long ago.

I'll kill those bastards!

I was screaming inside my head as I left Carly's house.

She had insisted she'd be fine—now that she was back out from her proverbial dark mental place—and after I'd promised to call her morning, lunch, and before bed.

It turned out my attempts at letting her know I was being followed last week, however valiant they might have been, had come too little, too late. Hunters had come to her house, looking for information. They wanted confirmation on if I had come into my powers. Carly had managed to make them think she had escaped and run away from the house, when she indeed only made her way up to her attic and hidden there. She'd feared if she didn't do that, and at least tried to get away from them, she'd lose me like she had my mother and father.

The hunters had come back later that first night, and the next few days following her disappearance. When they hadn't seen any sign of life within the house, they had enough of an answer, which kept them away, suspecting she'd run off on them. No one needed to tell me this was only a temporary fix.

By the time I arrived home, I had vowed to myself I would find this faction of hunters and be rid of them; that is, before they ever got to me. For whatever reason they chose to steal others' abilities, they would never succeed—not if I could help it. Because of this army of hunters, we've all been predominantly in hiding, and therefore, we knew nothing about what was really going on in the Fae world. To me, it seemed like we were prisoners on the edge of an upcoming battle between good versus evil—and left unprepared.

One thing I was sure of though…someone was going to have to talk to me sooner or later, because I wasn't one to get caught unawares. I just needed to figure out whom I could talk to, since Carly was a no-go according to my parents' own warnings.

RAFE

Payton had remained on my mind for the rest of the night as I headed home to work on family business. Paperwork never ended when one's business meant dealing and maintaining memberships and renewals, let alone all the other expenses and costs that came with running a gym.

Sleep came far too late, and once I'd found it, let's just say images of that woman's face haunted my subconscious and led to other visceral parts of my anatomy to waken, while all my body wanted to do was seek the ever so small amount of rest it needed to function.

Those lips were sin.

Her body had seemed to match the fire mine felt.

The question was: what would I do next when I saw her again?

With plans scrambling through my head and forming, I finally dozed off.

PAYTON

I opted for a sexy, figure-hugging, black tank dress and

covered my shoulders up with a white short-sleeved cardigan when my doorbell rang. I cursed the owner whose finger had dared to push that button.

Heading to the door to see who it was, I was more than vexed when I saw none other than Gage standing there.

On an exasperated huff, I asked, "What is it?"

"I wanted to talk to you about that guy you were with last night," he said.

"Gage, what goes on between Rafe and I isn't your business," I told him. "Listen, if you're looking for something to happen between us again, you're sadly mistaken."

"Why?" He seemed sad. "We were great together."

"Until you ruined it," I reminded him, while holding his gaze. "I don't regret what happened last weekend, but it's not going to happen again, nor am I going to come back to you."

"I need you, Payton," he begged. "I've been miserable without you." Taking a few steps toward me, he pulled me into him for a hug. I pushed him back, away from my door, and looked at his bereft face. Part of me wished I could simply forgive and forget, and be as happy as we once had been, but too much had happened with me between then and now. I was altogether a different person now. One with more secrets than she could ever imagine, and I couldn't help the fact that Rafe was on my mind incessantly since the day I had come into my succubus powers. Actually, more like from the moment we had laid eyes on each other in the club.

"This is goodbye, Gage," I announced and moved toward him. I was sure of my decision, confidence lacing my spoken words.

Taking his face into my hands, I moved in to kiss him on the lips. As soon as I felt his knees becoming weak, I pulled away, and looked at his bulging eyes. He'd fallen in that trance-like state, much like the first guy at the club a week ago, but I could tell he was still coherent. "You need to go." Closing the front door, I left him to recover from my assault on the front porch. I slid down with my back against the door, wrapping my arms around my knees only to finally hear him drive off in his car five minutes later.

It was now time for work.

I was less than enthusiastic to find myself surrounded by so many people. I knew tonight would at least be a slower night than yesterday, even though it was Saturday. I was thankful live bands only played one Friday a month.

Holly was back behind the bar when I got there.

"Hey," Joe greeted me when I walked into his office to drop my stuff off in one of the empty lockers. "Great job last night, by the way."

"Thanks."

"It's just you and Holly tonight. Let me know if you girls need any help, or if you run into trouble," he said.

"I'm sure we'll be fine, but I'll keep you updated," I told him.

I couldn't have been more right—for once.

The night flew by and aside from my succubus charms, which continuously attracted all kinds of men my way— enticing them with my looks only to turn them away disappointed—I found myself actually having fun.

Holly and I had found our rhythm, and everything seemed to flow. Tonight had been slightly more bearable from an empath standpoint as well. I had been able to keep my block up longer, which could explain the calm collected feelings deep within me.

The one thing that bothered me was the feeling of disappointment, which increased ever so slightly as the night went on; noticing Rafe hadn't come in. After last night, that kiss, I was hoping to see him again. I needed to know why he hadn't been affected in the same way as everyone else by my charms—or was that perception a figment of my imagination? Those bright sapphire eyes of his did manage to make me feel like my troubles melted away when he was around. The more I thought about it, the more I was convinced he was Fae. I just didn't know for sure, nor did I intend on bringing up the subject until I had further justification to my suspicions, but it was simply just that—an inkling.

"Hey, Reid! Turn it up, will ya?" Holly ordered.

Reid was one of the club's most infamous DJs. After everyone had left, it was simply him, Holly, Joe, and I left for cleanup. Dancing to the rhythm as we mopped the floors, washed the glassware, and restocked the fridges with the necessary liquor, we had loads of fun, not to mention, a few laughs. It was hard to believe it was now nearing three in the morning.

I was glad when Holly offered to drive me home. My feet were killing me tonight and my bed beckoned my undivided attention. After thanking her for the ride, I let myself into the house.

I didn't make it halfway from the entryway to the stairwell when arms wrapped around my neck, restraining me into a choke hold. My hands clutched at the large arm that held me with no regard for the discomfort I was in.

"Come with us and you'll be fine," I heard his boisterous voice in my ear.

Right then I'd made the decision to refuse to go down without a fight.

Stomping on my assailant's foot and shoving an elbow strategically in his gut, I wanted to bet he'd rue the day he decided to try to take me for his own, in my house no less. As I turned to face my intruder, I realized this dude was quite large, and I was surprised I had that much of an effect on him physically.

He smirked. "Good. I was hoping you'd put up a little bit of a fight."

That's when I saw the glint of a switchblade in his hand. Suddenly, I began regretting my decision to fight back. With one swipe of his bladed grip, I knew this wasn't going to end well. He slashed a mark on my left forearm. Clutching at my burning wound, eyeing the crimson blade, I somehow managed to remember something my father had told me about size and agility.

Payton, remember the smallest are quickest and the larger fall harder.

The goon might have been blocking my path to the front door, but I knew this house like the back of my hand, something I prayed he didn't. Who knows how long he'd been lying in wait for me?

Despite being slightly injured, I knew I was able to get myself out of this situation. So long as I kept my head straight. For once, I was thankful my father had taught me some self-defense and basic martial arts, despite my numerous bouts of complaining. He had thought it wise, since I was in the know about my fate and what I might have to do eventually, that I be thoroughly prepared. I know what you're going to say. This comes off like something out of a Lara Croft movie. No—I'm no treasure seeking, tomb-raiding vixen but her outfits did rock.

Snap out of it!

After dodging him a few more advances, I managed to trip the bastard up with a floor roundhouse kick and made a rush for the front door, only to find myself face-to-face with some other hunter moron.

This guy was slightly smaller than the first.

"How many of you are there?" I asked sarcastically, kicking him backward in the gut with a smirk on my face.

I must have been too slow or perhaps, a little overly cocky about my abilities because he grabbed and twisted my ankle, pulling up as my already unstable footing was lost. I ended up flat on my back on the floor, my head throbbing from the hard contact it made with the ceramic tile of the foyer. Before my eyes began to roll into the back of my head, I witnessed the guy who had caused my fall take a tumble down. I smiled as darkness took me. Help had miraculously arrived.

My head felt like it was about to explode, the smell of the air was sweet, and the feeling beneath my body was soft; not like that of a cold ceramic-tiled floor. That's when my eyes snapped open and I took in a very unfamiliar room.

This isn't much of a hostage situation, I thought to myself as I sat up on the rather comfortable sofa, noticing my bandaged arm.

"Oh good, you're up!" Rafe said as he came to kneel down in front of me, putting a glass of water on the coffee table next to him.

"Where am I?" I whispered, clutching at the back of my head, finding a slight bump.

Ouch!

"Here." He gave me a couple of ibuprofen and I popped them in my mouth, gladly accepting the glass of water he handed me to wash the pills down.

"What the hell happened?" I asked.

"I got rid of two goons for you, that's what," he said, grabbing my face in his hands. "I brought you to my place because I knew they wouldn't bother us here."

"What do you mean *they*?" I asked, eyeing him attentively.

He shrugged his shoulders. "They knew where you lived. Your place was trashed, so I locked it up and brought you where I knew you'd be safe." I nodded in comprehension. Feeling guilty for thinking he knew more than he was letting on, I averted my eyes from him. "Look at me," he requested softly. He seemed to study my eyes for a moment. "It doesn't look like you have a concussion, but I think you should try and stay awake."

"Oh, so you're a doctor now?" He smirked at my sarcasm. "And how do you propose I manage to stay awake? It's got to be going on four o'clock in the morning by now. I don't think…" His twinkling eyes full of mischief had my voice trailing off.

"I can think of something," he said suggestively, and I knew where his mind had headed.

I couldn't help but blush at his innuendo, the memory of last night still lingering fresh in my mind.

"So you'll talk me out of the danger zone, huh?" I feigned innocence.

"If that's what you want, sure," he said breathlessly against the skin next to my ear, causing an exciting shiver to run down the front of my body. "But I think you know what I meant." He pulled away to look at me, as I gulped back the sudden abundance of saliva that had deliciously filled my mouth in anticipation. My emotions were in overdrive, and I was sure it was all thanks to the old succubus powers that be.

Holy shit! I thought as he softly pressed his lips against mine and a rush of heat seeped through my body.

How does he do that?

CHAPTER 8

RAFE

Fuck! How does she do that?

With just a simple innocent look, the woman could bring any man down to his knees. Case in point, here I was—on my knees—my lips pressed to hers in a tender gesture of care, while my body was telling me to maul her.

Getting to my feet, I pulled away, hovering above the beauty strewn over my couch, then proceeded to lower myself so I could lay down. She moved in tandem to make room for me, then pulled me so I was above her, her hands sliding under the edge of my T-shirt.

Silk.

So fucking soft.

My dick would have permanent indentations from the zipper on my jeans by the night's end, I was sure of it.

Burying my nose in the crook of her neck, I nuzzled the warm skin, then gave her a slight nip. The mewl that came out of her resembled that of a cat in heat.

So I continued…

PAYTON

My senses were in overdrive and all I cared about was quenching my every desire with all things Rafe, at the moment. His hands glided over the skin of my arms, causing wonderful electrical currents to be exchanged between us as he hovered over me.

My hands had found themselves under his shirt, massaging the rippling muscles hidden there while he kissed my neck, eliciting tingles that floated down to my toes. With a delicate nip to the sweet spot below my ear, he made those tingling toes of mine curl, causing a lustful moan to escape my lips.

He pulled away to gaze into my eyes where I knew he saw the look of urgency. I witnessed the brightness of his glaze over and change into slightly darker pools, flecks of gold swimming about until he brought his face back down to me; exacting I met him, kiss for kiss, touch for touch, our passions intertwining with one another.

His hand streamed down and gently massaged a breast before moving down to my thigh, which at this point, I had realized was completely bare, seeing as my dress had risen up with the way my legs were bent and hugging the sides of his hips.

"How do you do what you do to me?" he whispered over my lips, in between kisses, and I couldn't help the sexy giggle that tumbled out of my throat.

"What do you mean?" I nipped at his collarbone, giving him time to breathe and respond.

"I normally don't do this so quickly," he explained.

"I have that effect it seems," I said, trailing my kisses up to his jaw, pausing to lick his bottom lip, which caused a guttural rumbling to come from his throat. "We can stop, if you want. But if it makes you feel any better," I paused to look at him, "I don't do this either." Then I closed the gap between us again.

When Rafe pulled away, I knew that look and was convinced of what he felt. He was conflicted—torn, as was I—between our physical urges and what felt right, but also by our regular personal beliefs.

"Thing is, I don't want to stop," he announced, so sure of his urges he continued his invasion on my body. "I don't think I could even if I wanted to," he added against the skin above my breasts.

"Mmm…" was all I could manage, as his hand reached to the heat between my legs, causing my body to tremble and arch into his, needing more from him.

If I thought the release I had felt at my ex's hand was heavenly, it was nothing compared to what I had witnessed being at the mercy of Rafe and his sinfully cunning craft.

The thought of how he had me writhing in multiple bursts of pleasure sent waves of heat throughout my body as I lay there, draped over half of his body, molded to him, as he traced circles on the side of my shoulder with his fingertips. Daylight was beginning to penetrate the living room through the partially closed curtains, basking us in the rays of the early morning sun.

"Are you awake?" he whispered down, fanning his sweet breath on my face.

"Mmm…" I mumbled, not caring to move from my nest within his chest.

I knew I had to get up some time. Reality dictated my very existence, and as much as I wanted this moment to last, predetermined obligations beckoned me.

Taking a deep breath, I positioned myself to get up but found Rafe tightening his grip around my shoulders and back, holding me even closer to him.

"Where do you think you're going?" he asked.

"Home?" I said this with a questioning tone, as if I was

now asking him for permission. He thought it amusing, judging by the low chuckle he let out.

"Not without me, you're not," he argued, with a bemused smirk.

"Hero complex?" I laughed slightly as he nodded his response. "Just as well. I wouldn't mind the company."

"Is that all I am?" he teased. "I thought I'd serve as a distraction." He tilted my chin so he could give me another one of his epic soft kisses. One that momentarily made me forget my train of thought. "Don't think I can't sense the effects I have on you, Payton."

I smiled at him sweetly, as I let the proverbial fog dissipate from my head. "What effects?" I innocently laughed, feigning his influence wasn't that grand, but leaving it obvious still he did indeed hold some power over me.

"I'll remind you when the time is right." He smirked before kissing the tip of my nose.

An hour later, we were in Rafe's car, driving to my house. I looked out the passenger side window, pondering what state my home, my sanctuary, would look like when I got there.

"Everything will be okay," he said, putting a hand on my bare thigh, rubbing his thumb in a circular pattern, which managed to shoo my dark thoughts away.

"I hope so," I said softly, almost at a whisper.

RAFE

I dreaded her reaction when she saw the state of her home. I'd taken the time to do a walk-around before leaving.

Her entire main entrance was in shambles. There were a few holes in the walls and some small pieces of furniture had been overturned; some broken beyond repair and others salvageable.

I wish I'd had the time to clean things up for her, but playing maid wasn't part of my job description.

I only hoped she'd take things in stride, like she had with the rest of her life before now, and rally up her optimism in order to move on. And if I could, I'd do it unbeknownst to her, at her side.

PAYTON

Rafe had let me go upstairs to change, opting for a shower beforehand—I went about my daily routine, as if no one was here—knowing he wouldn't mind. He made me feel safe.

Letting go of the aches, pains, and negativity from the previous night, I let the scalding hot water rain down over my body. I never noticed the sexy male who watched me lather myself clean, until I reached for my towel only to find it absent from its hook.

"Looking for this?" Rafe asked.

Letting the steam clear enough for me to make out the smug look on his face, he handed me the towel. Flustered, I grabbed it and quickly wrapped it around myself, making sure I had tucked it in tight at my bust. It didn't matter that only hours before, he'd had his hands and mouth all over me, and had brought me to orgasm multiple times with only his palm and digits.

Feeling secure, or composed rather, I turned to find Rafe standing right there, a hungry look in his eyes.

"Distraction?" I smirked at him.

"I'd say I'm sorry for catching you off guard, but that wouldn't be honest of me," he confessed, pulling me out of the shower stall so I stood pressed against his chest.

"And here I thought I was the seductress." I sighed for dramatics, then moaned when his lips found my collarbone.

"That you are," he whispered against my flushed skin, feeling whatever small amount of resolve in me dissipate.

Letting my arms wrap around his neck, he slowly walked me backward until I felt the edge of the bed hit me behind the knees. Was I finally going to find out the magic the rest of his body was capable of making me feel? His hand had been nothing more than too obliging last night.

The doorbell ringing was the furthest thing I anticipated hearing at this point in time. Refusing to put a stop to this moment of bliss we were sharing, I kissed him harder, demanding more from him. I pulled up on his shirt as he let me slide it over his head, my towel beginning to loosen.

Ding. Dong.

Ignoring the door again, I let Rafe straighten up and slip out of his pants before taking me into his strong arms and lowering us to my bed slowly. My towel falling away from my front—leaving me completely bare—was the furthest thing from my mind when my hands wandered south of his border and found what I so desperately desired.

RAFE

I could feel the urgency of her hunger for me without even touching her. It's as though her body emanated some kind of magnetic field, pulling me in.

Her eyes held me in a trance.

Fuck!

Her delicate fingers slipped into my briefs, surrounding my cock, lightly pumping it before it came to a stop.

"I need you, Rafe," she whispered her confession. The raw truth was written across her face.

"Then you'll have me," I promised, then leaned down to take her lips with mine.

I'd have given her anything in that moment.

Shimmying my underwear down my legs, I trailed my lips down to her collarbone, between her breasts, and lower to her stomach, stopping to blow a puff of air on her clean-shaven bits.

Something primal came over me with the scent of her bodywash mixing with her arousal.

"I need to taste you," I growled.

Her head bobbed up and down with urgency. "Please."

"Fuck, but you're tight," I muttered, circling her clit with my tongue, two fingers slipping inside, rubbing in just that right spot I knew would set her off as it had earlier.

"Oh, shit!" she cried out, as I felt the first of her spasms. "Fuck!"

Her juices coated my face, but the minute I brought myself over to watch her as she recovered from her climax, she pulled me down and kissed me senseless.

"Mmm…More," she demanded, then reached down for my cock and pulled my hips closer.

"Wait." I ground my teeth. It would be a miracle if I lasted five minutes at this point. "Condom."

I shifted toward the edge of the bed, my ass in the air as I fished for my jeans. I know, attractive, right? But the giggle and playful smack to my ass had me moving in a hurry. Finding the rubber, I kneeled between Payton's splayed legs and sheathed myself, before moving into her waiting arms. The look of pure lust she gave as she saw me handling my junk had me thinking up ideas on how to explore this exhibitionist move at some point.

Christ, but this is like coming home.

The moment I'd seated myself inside her, I knew my life had changed forever.

PAYTON

I could have sworn the house shook at the peak of our explosive climax.

Rafe rolled over to the mattress, as our bodies glistened with sweat, our breathing labored. It was at this point I realized my marking was now burning. Not a painful heated burn, but one that felt almost freezing cold. Giving it a quick glance, I realized it had evolved yet again—and it sort of glowed.

What the hell? A third marking?

I'd never had that reaction before with my other two markings either. The odd thing is, I felt as though I had reached the end of something. What—I had no clue—but I aimed to find out.

Terrified of being found out about this newest development, I immediately jumped to sit upright and reached for my towel to cover up.

Rafe grabbed my arm, pulling me back down beside him. "What's going on?" he asked, studying my face for some answer I was terrified of giving. He was quite the perceptive man.

I'll have to be careful with this one, I told myself.

"Just got cold, is all," I said, smiling sheepishly, hoping he wasn't about to call me on my bluff.

"Come here." He pulled me closer onto him, wrapping his arms around me, as he rubbed my back.

A sigh escaped my lips as I felt myself relax and contentment filled me to the brim. There'd be a time to worry about all of this supernatural business later.

It wasn't hard to convince me to pack a bag to spend the night at Rafe's. I had told him I would as long as we stopped by Carly's, first. Joe had given me the night off after he heard what had happened after my shift. With the way I was still hurting, I couldn't have been more thrilled at the idea of losing money for once, or spending time with a man who seemed to want me just as much as I wanted him.

I entered Carly's with the help of the key she had given me, leaving Rafe in his car. I was happy she had stuck to her guns and kept all of her windows and doors locked.

"Carly?" I called out for her.

My aunt peeked around the corner to the entrance of her kitchen. She rushed over to give me a quick hug, and then I felt her go rigid in my arms.

"Rafael?" she said while letting go of me.

I turned to look at him and then back to Carly. So the man can give direction but apparently doesn't take it all too well.

"You two know each other?" I asked, confused.

"Uh…" Rafe hesitated; long enough for me to start thinking a multitude of things, none of them good I assure you.

"Payton!" Carly said loudly, as she noticed the look of horror strewn across my face. My head snapped up to her as she started to laugh. "Relax, honey. It's not like that." Relief swept over me. Could you blame me for thinking the worst? Carly's only a few years older than I am, and like a typical succubus: she was hot. "You should sit down though," she announced.

"I'm not sitting down until you tell me what's going on," I told her, turning to look at Rafe. "Both of you."

Nearly an hour later, I was trying to digest everything

Carly had just divulged. It was all beginning to make sense to me now; well, some of it. From the day of my twenty-first birthday to this very minute, the puzzle pieces were starting to be placed. Carly knew a hell of a lot more than she had been letting on. Don't get me wrong, I'm still pissed. I felt betrayed by Carly, but part of me understood why I hadn't been privy to this information. It all boiled down to my safety. But Rafe had some serious explaining to do.

"What's your story?" I turned to ask Rafe, my arms crossed at my chest.

"You have to know I seriously had no intention of falling for you," he began.

My heart sank.

He's falling?

"How could you have fallen for me? We don't even know each other," I blurted out with a frustrated huff, despite the fact I knew what he meant all along. Honestly, if I was willing to admit it just then, I think part of me had already fallen for him too. Hell, I wouldn't have let him take my V-card if I hadn't been feeling the same way. "And…"

"Payton!" Carly interrupted, and my head snapped back to her, my face red with frustration more than anger. "Listen to what he has to say, please," she finished softly.

"Fine." I nodded my head toward Rafe, indicating him to keep talking.

"I didn't think I would fall, but your pull on me is too much. I'm supposed to be able to resist that," he explained.

Resist?

"I was supposed to keep an eye on you, make sure you were kept safe. Help you out. Then get lost."

Resist?

My thoughts were stuck on that statement, and the thought from the other day about me wondering why it was he wasn't succumbing to my kisses of death like all the others, as of late.

"So you would in essence, use, abuse, and then ditch?" I asked hotly.

"No! It's not like that at all, Payton, and you know that! I didn't lie when I told you I don't do that ever," he told me, then sucked in a deep breath, rubbing the back of his neck. "Assistance, that's all I was to provide; but you…You got to me. I was simply assigned to watch over you, not spend time with you."

I sat there in silence, not sure what to say next. Heck, I wasn't sure what I was supposed to be thinking. All I knew was what he meant by me getting to him. He had gotten to me too, and no matter what my views on physical intimacy were, they were thrown out the window when it came to him. The pull between us had been too great to ignore. It still was.

"What Rafe's saying is that he didn't ask for what happened between you two. Our families have known of one another for as long as the lines have existed, Payton. I don't think any of the elders had foreseen the possibility, that down the line, the Nottinghams and Devonshires were to unite." Carly's eyes bored into mine, pleading me to make sense of it all, and I was.

"So you're…" My voice trailed softly as my gaze found Rafe's.

"I'm Fae, Payton," he whispered, as though it was a secret between the three of us. "Didn't you wonder why your kisses barely weakened me?"

I shrugged. "I thought it was my mind playing tricks on me."

"They would weaken anyone out there but me," he explained. "Like you, I'm a hybrid." My mouth formed an 'o' shape in comprehension.

"Where's your tattoo?" The words left my mouth

before I realized what I had asked, for reasons unknown other than skepticism at his revelation.

He peeled his T-shirt up, over his head, turned his back to me and I found myself blushing. There, in its glory, was the ancient triskel symbol.

My feet began to walk up to him of their own accord, my fingers aiming to trail the lightly raised piece of flesh, which felt cool to the touch, as mine did earlier. His breath caught as soon as my fingers made contact with his skin.

"What are you?" I asked, "or do I even want to know?"

"You should know. Part of it, I think you've already figured out by now, based on our attraction. Firstly, I possess the power to change people's minds; secondly, I'm from a long line of defenders…or watchers, sworn to protect the heir of the ancient families, ensuring descendants; and third…"

"I thought you said you were a hybrid?" I backed up a few steps.

"I am. You, Payton, have given me a third. I'm an incubus. That is something entirely new and was revealed to me the day I first touched you."

"You've known what I was since the day I collapsed?" I asked him.

He shook his head and my look of bewilderment made him chuckle. "I've known of you my entire life. I just didn't know about being matched with you specifically, until that day you're speaking of," he explained.

"So how do I know you haven't used your power of persuasion on me then?" I asked, skeptical of the feelings that had overwhelmed me when he and I were alone together.

"I know it isn't much, but all you have is my word on that one." He looked at me, and for some reason, I knew he wasn't lying. "I can only alter someone's way of thinking or decision when their minds aren't one-hundred-percent made up, and I certainly can't alter my match's perception of me or their decisions."

Turning my back to the both of them, my feet took me toward the front of the house. I was no longer in full control of my body, my legs moving of their own accord.

"I need to go," I announced and kept walking. "Carly, we're not done here," I said over my shoulder.

Heavy footsteps made to follow behind me and I knew it was Rafe.

"Leave her," Carly whispered.

I couldn't stop analyzing all the information I had obtained in such a short amount of time.

Savior to my damsel in distress.

Incubus to my succubus.

Mind melder to my empath.

Matched.

What the hell does that even mean?

THE END

ABOUT THE AUTHOR

Born and raised in small town Northern Ontario, Canada, Carey Decevito has always had a penchant for reading and writing.

More than a decade later, with weeks of sleepless nights, she finally gave in and put pen to paper (more like fingers to keyboard!) She submitted to the dreams that plagued her. And the rest, as they say, is history!

A member of the RWA, Carey enjoys spending time with family and friends, the outdoors, travelling, and playing tourist in Canada's National Capital region. When life gets crazy, this contemporary erotic romance author seeks respite through her writing and reading. If all else fails, she knows there's never a dull moment with her two daughters, her goofy husband, and cat and dog who she swears are out to get her.

She is the author of both *The Broken Men Chronicles*, *Nightshade* and *Essence Extracted* series.

CONNECT ONLINE

Website – www.careydecevito.com
Email – carey.decevito@gmail.com
Facebook – http://www.facebook.com/carey.writes

ALSO BY
CAREY DECEVITO

The Broken Men Chronicles series

Once Written, Twice Shy
Almost Forgotten
Play Me to Infinity
To Forgive & Hold Safe
A Heart's War

Nightshade series

Night Break
Night Shift

Essence Extracted Trilogy

Essence Derived

once written twice shy

THE BROKEN MEN CHRONICLES

book one

excerpt

carey decevito

PROLOGUE

I stared at the overly large bags that lay by the front entrance with what must have been the world's largest *what the fuck* look on my face.

"I can't do this anymore," she said.

Her words tore me to shreds.

"What do you mean you *can't do this anymore*? Julie, you haven't been doing anything to fix *this*."

"I'm done, Paxton."

I ran my hands through my hair, pulling at the handful of blond tresses gripped between my rigid fingers. The prickle in my scalp did enough to keep my temper in check and diffuse some of my anger. "You've got to be kidding me."

I couldn't believe it, but then again, part of me could.

She was giving up on everything.

My love, our life, our family; it had all disappeared in the blink of an eye.

I still loved her, but in all honesty, I can also state that I haven't been in love with her for quite some time.

We've been together for nearly five years. In that time, we had built a home; one that was graced with our beautiful three-year-old son, Jasper.

My hand ran down my face.

Christ, how am I going to explain this to Jasper?

I was willing to try and work things out. Hell, I'd even mentioned marriage counseling on multiple occasions, but like everything else, work came first and the sessions she'd promised had never materialized.

I looked up at the woman who stood in the entrance to what I had considered our home; frustration, anger, bitterness, and that subtle feeling of failure were all too overwhelming. "Fine," I said. "But what about Jasper?"

"Can you keep him for this week? It's just until I get situated. We can discuss custody later."

"Where are you going?"

"Todd asked me to move in with him," she said as if I'd known about her relationship with the man the entire time. I'd suspected she'd maintained her infidelity but I didn't know for sure until now.

I huffed. "So he's still in the picture." I hadn't asked, so much as accused her. She nodded. "How long have you two been–" I couldn't finish the sentence.

Bile rose from my stomach.

"Does it matter?"

"You can go," I said in a defeated tone. I looked down at my feet when all I wanted to do is ask her what happened to *can we try and work things out?* I groaned at the memory and shook it out of my head in dismay. "Get out."

"Pax–" She made to step toward me with an outstretched hand.

I shook my head to stop her, my blood pressure rising with her lack of departure. "I said *get out*!" I pointed toward the door, my stomach contents churning further.

The woman took off like a bat out of hell.

And that was it.

I was tired of having a one-sided relationship and was thus relieved at the woman's departure.

The news of her continued adultery had shocked me, especially when she had sworn to make an effort to sort things out between us. It explained why we had remained in our separate rooms all of this time, living our lives apart as though we were roommates. It more than proved that we were better off without each other. This was really the end of my marriage.

When I married, I had intended it to be for life.

Well, I guess life had a plan of its own, huh?

With each passing day, I picked up the broken pieces of me. I hadn't realized that I had stifled so much of myself over the years to try and please a woman that seemed to never be sated with anything I said or did.

Fueled by my feelings of loss and neglect, I made a decision, which led me to rediscover an old love.

The proverbial flame was rekindled and I began to write again.

For what felt like an eternity, I wrote. When I was done, I read my piece over so many times that my words no longer made sense, forcing me to put it down and go back to it later.

I stared at my finished manuscript displayed on my screen. *What am I going to do with this?*

I had discovered a site, a few months before. It had been recommended by a colleague. The venue allowed people from around the world to peruse and read various works written by amateurs. Some of the work on there I found horrid, while others, despite their various grammatical and punctual flaws, you wished you could set your hands on an edited and printed copy, they were so great.

What the hell?

I decided to chance it.

With a bit of copy and paste, and a little restructuring, I hit the *publish* button and there it was. My first written piece was out for the world to see.

It wasn't until a few months after I had posted my work that I stumbled upon a comment that I couldn't dismiss. I ached for constructive feedback, but the lack of it was getting to me due to the site being overrun by teenagers. I debated getting rid of my profile altogether up until that fateful day.

That short message was where things began to change for me. With simple words of appreciation, intellectual and heartfelt thoughts, followed by a click of her mouse, Alissa had made me smile.

I sought her profile out and found that she was a fellow amateur writer just like me.

She's gorgeous, had been my first impression. Despite her evident beauty, something else could be seen in her profile photo; something that beckoned me further, begged my curiosity to look beyond the surface. It was in her eyes.

Loneliness.

Or was I reading into things too much, since I was such a novice at these social media-like sites?

For a few weeks, I sat on Alissa's words alone as I read through some of her work.

She was good.

Better than good even.

I thought that I'd end up with one of those written numbers that didn't make much sense or that glittered in the night featuring vampires and werewolves. Boy was I wrong!

The woman sure knew how to paint a vivid picture. She pulled off the hot and sexy but kept it real all at once by adding emotion, drama, even a bit of action and suspense to her mix. Her work was altogether something reminiscent of everyday life: the good, the bad, the ugly, the… Well, you get the picture.

A few days after reading her last novel, a dream influenced

by her work prompted me to finally write out an acknowledgment to her comment.

From there, we began to chat through private messages on a near daily basis.

We never stopped…

CHAPTER 1

Just short of a year later...

Waiting in the airport terminal, I couldn't remember the last time I had felt like this. The anxiety that consumed me was reminiscent of my first date with my first girlfriend as a teenager.

I looked up at the screen and saw that US Airways flight 2583 to Jacksonville, North Carolina had landed. In a matter of minutes, Alissa would be standing before me in the flesh. My thoughts flittered to that first day, nearly a year ago, when we first made contact.

The conveyer belt that carried the luggage snapped me out of my reverie when it ceased moving and the area around me had become deserted.

Had something gone wrong, had she stood me up?

I lowered myself to the bench behind me and let my head drop into my hands. I sighed. "Serves you right for thinking she'd show," I mumbled.

I was trying to convince myself that I should leave when I felt a soft hand on my shoulder. "Paxton?" a soft-spoken woman said at my side, her voice familiar from our numerous phone calls and Skype conversations.

She's here.

My heart thumped out of my chest. I felt foolish for thinking the worse and excited that I was proven wrong. I got up to face Alissa, who had a beaming smile splayed on her face. Boy was that smile contagious! My lips tugged upward instantly.

She let out a giggle and after dropping her bag, she jumped me with a hug. Without hesitation, my arms found their way around her waist to return her enthusiastic greeting.

"You looked like a man deep in thought."

I set her back but held on to the sides of her arms. "Can I be honest?"

I breathed easier when she nodded, "I wouldn't expect anything less from you."

I shrugged my shoulders sheepishly and averted my gaze from her momentarily before eying her. "I thought you weren't coming."

She looked as if I'd slapped her.

"Paxton, I would have called or emailed. Hell, I would have messaged you if anything had come up. We've talked about meeting for months. I wouldn't–"

Call it insanity or whatever you will, I did the only thing my brain could process at the time and took the one step toward her. Standing toe-to-toe, I let go of her arms, grabbed her face and crashed my lips to hers in an effort to shut her up. What was most surprising was how natural the act felt.

Her hand flew to her mouth as soon as I pulled back, eyes wide. No big surprise that I hadn't been the only one shocked at my actions.

Where had this sudden forwardness come from? Maybe it had been the relief that she was finally standing before me in person. Maybe it was that she'd proved, with her flustered rambling, that I hadn't been the only one looking forward our meeting.

Yes, things had gotten personal with our countless chats. But despite the numerous times we had flirted, exchanged photos, talked dirty, and even discussed how she had come up with some of the steamy scenes from her stories, I worried that I had crossed a line.

Even when this feels completely natural.

"Alissa, I'm–"

She shook her head and lifted her hand. "I knew that was coming at one point or another. I just didn't expect…" With a small upward quirk of her lips, she waved her hand in a dismissive gesture. "Never mind. That was nice."

I instantly breathed easier and grabbed her carry-on luggage. "Let's get out of here." I offered her my hand to hold. "Assuming you're still up for it, after my mauling you and all."

She giggled nervously but grasped my proffered grip in hers. I walked us out of luggage claim toward the parking structure with a certainty that I hadn't screwed things up so quick out of the gate, but maintained a level of wariness nonetheless.

W ith her luggage stowed in the back of my SUV, I headed to open the passenger side door for her.

If I'm going to be honest, my mind was presently stuck on our brief kiss.

Apparently I wasn't the only one.

Before I knew what hit me, Alissa had me pinned against the side of my vehicle, her body and lips smashed against mine.

My hands reached for her hips, pulling her into me as I licked her bottom lip, begging for entrance. The small taste of her in luggage claim had proven one thing—that I wanted more and as long as she was handing out samples, I wasn't going to decline her offer.

With a light moan, she granted me access while her hands found their way around my neck and into my hair. We breathed each other in.

Alissa pulled away first, her chest heaving for air. I was none the better. The woman knew how to kiss. So much so that a certain part of my anatomy had begun to stir with that more thorough taste of her.

Don't judge, it's been a while.

She hid her face in my chest.

I pecked the top of her head. "I guess we're even, huh?" She groaned, making me chuckle. I grabbed her chin, tilting it to reveal a beautiful crimson. A chaste press of my lips to hers seemed to alleviate her sudden embarrassment. "Let's get going." But that flush of colour in her cheeks was so becoming I simply had to tease her. "I can't have you all over me for everyone to see." I winked. Her blush had barely begun to fade as my words caused it to flare up once more, gaining me the reaction I was looking for. "I love that look on you by the way."

She waited for me to get behind the wheel before asking, "What look?"

"Your blush," I said and buckled myself in. "I know you told me about it but it's nothing like I had pictured. You're gorgeous."

She clasped her cheeks with her hands in an effort to conceal another wave of red and failing miserably. "You need to stop that."

In a mocked tone of innocence I said, "What?" I leaned over the middle console to flick her nose with an index finger. "It's true."

A soft laugh escaped her and she nodded toward the steering wheel. "Get to driving, will you?"

I dropped her luggage as soon as we crossed the threshold. Kicking the door shut, I pulled Alissa so her back was against my chest and hugged her from behind, setting my chin on her shoulder and savoring the feel of her against me.

A perfect fit.

"I can't believe you're actually here. You hungry?" It was nearly dinnertime and although I'd had a late lunch, my stomach grumbled.

She giggled at the noise. "A little." She wrapped her arms over mine. "What do you have in mind?"

I'm no culinary savant or anything, but I'm not the type of person to cook until I set fire to my kitchen either.

Until tonight apparently.

Part of it was Alissa's fault, despite the fact that she would beg to differ.

With a faltering grip, white powder filled the room after she recommended I use either cornstarch or flour to thicken the gravy. Flour, as it turns out, was all I had.

A fit of laughter consumed us as we attempted to clean up, making more of a mess out of ourselves than anything else.

She proceeded to wipe at me with a damp tea towel. When she got a little too close to a certain area, I grabbed her wrist to stop her. I pulled the cloth from her grip and wiped at her face while I felt her cool fingers wiping at mine.

Our eyes connected and locked.

Our laughter subsided.

The braised pork chops and boiling potatoes forgotten, we found ourselves wrapped in each other like a pair of randy teenagers. There was no telling who had started it. The chemistry was instantaneous.

When we came up for air, Alissa said, "Is it me or is it getting hot in here?"

As soon as she'd said it, something captured my attention from the corner of my eye, making me turn to look.

Our indulgence had resulted in the potatoes becoming an over-boiled pile of mush. The braised chops were charred, as the pan had caught fire. And the gravy did thicken—to the consistency of a dried up hockey puck stuck to the bottom of its pot.

Suffice it to say, dinner was effectively ruined.

Alissa was giggling into my back as I managed to put a stop to the tiny blaze with the help of a box of baking soda and an expired kitchen fire extinguisher.

Taking a deep breath, and looking over my shoulder at the woman still trying to gain her composure I asked her, "How do you feel about take-out?"

"I think it's a safer bet."

CHAPTER 2

When the kitchen was tidied up, the pots having been left to soak in the sink, and our food ordered, I offered Alissa a shower.

"You go ahead," she said. "I'll take mine after."

"I've got two bathrooms. You can use the one in my room since this is where you'll be staying. I'll take–"

"I can't kick you out," she said. "I could–"

"I didn't want to assume anything and I wanted you to be comfortable. The spare room doesn't have a bed yet, so I'll take the pullout couch. It's fine." I nodded toward the en suite bathroom. "Go ahead, it's through there. I'll take the main bath down the hall."

In a rush to get cleaned up and return to Alissa, I was fresh out of the shower when I realized that I hadn't grabbed any clean clothes to change into.

I wrapped the towel around my waist and headed out to gather something to put on.

Just as I slipped into my room, hoping to make a quick exit without being caught, I was graced with a sight that made my heart stop and start up again at a staccato pace.

Bent over, rummaging through her bag for what I

presumed was a shirt, Alissa's heart shaped ass, covered in a tight pair of blue jeans, was facing me along with her blonde locks dripping down her back.

I took a step forward and hadn't expected the floorboards to creak, giving my presence away.

She stood up ramrod straight and whirled around to face me, grabbing the first thing out of her bag to cover herself with.

I looked at it and burst out laughing. "You might need something more than that, sweetheart."

Her eyes looked down in horror when she found herself clutching a black lace bra. Blushing, her mouth opened as if to say something but nothing came out. Instead, I saw her gaze moving up my towel-clad torso, to my chest, her head tilting to the side, eyes widening, and her breathing picked up.

Grabbing her discarded towel, she quickly covered up and said, "I think I'm just going to–" She started to make a quick dash for the hallway with a mortified look on her face.

My hand clasped her arm to stop her. "Let me just grab the few things I didn't earlier and get out of here."

Turning away from her, I searched through my closet and pulled the few items I needed and headed for the exit. "I'll see you when you're done." I paused at the bedroom door before leaving her. "Has anyone ever told you that you're hot when you're flustered?"

I didn't wait for a response. A few steps down the hall, I could hear the woman grumbling to herself and smiled. Things were definitely far from boring with Alissa around.

The pizza arrived while Alissa was still getting herself straightened out. I figured that she was done by now but that she was dealing with some residual embarrassment before coming downstairs to join me. In the short amount of time since her arrival, I had come to think of her meek demeanor as a rather endearing quality of hers.

I poured some wine for us after getting the plates ready, knowing that she wouldn't be that much longer.

I smiled as I replayed the earlier series of events in my head.

Like any normal hot-blooded male out there, I'd be crazy if I said I didn't want to get laid by the woman currently holed up in my bedroom. We had chemistry, there was no denying that, but the gentleman in me urged me to slow things down a bit. There was something greater to lose here; a friendship that I wasn't willing to part with.

And maybe something greater?

The couch dipped beside me and the wine in my goblet sloshed about, bringing me back to the present.

"So, I guess you didn't lie when you said you knew how to make a towel look good, huh?" She smirked.

I eyed her amused face, surprised at her overtness and humored all the same. "I deserve that. I'm sorry for barging in. I–"

She placed a hand on my arm and squeezed lightly. "It's okay. You just took me by surprise."

"Here." I handed over her glass of wine, watching as she took a large gulp of the Cabernet Sauvignon. Trying to get my head back in the game had proved useless with my next statement. "For what it's worth, those jeans look fantastic but I have to confess that my imagination is running wild with pictures of you wearing that black lace bra you were holding on to."

She laughed. "Boy, you're a cheeky one, aren't you?"

I smiled, happy that our familiar playful banter from our online conversations had begun to creep into our face-to-face setting as time went on. I was starting to see more of the Alissa I had grown to know over the last ten months. Witnessing a genuine physical reaction instead of those stupid emoticon faces or some video rendition of her was a refreshing change.

I was able to read her like one of her books, and what I took in only made me want to be around her more. There was a level of comfort between us that I hadn't seen coming, despite our few moments of awkwardness.

After dinner, I noticed Alissa fighting off the urge to fall asleep as our movie went on, so I pulled her legs on top of my lap in order to let her stretch out and be more comfortable.

When the credits began to roll, I turned the TV off and lifted the sleeping woman into my arms. By instinct, her arms wrapped themselves around my neck. Nuzzling against my jaw, Alissa mumbled something indiscernible while I carried her to my bedroom.

I set her down on my bed and tried to pull back but she woke and latched onto my shirt, capturing me with those cerulean eyes of hers.

I froze.

"Please don't go," she whispered and pulled me down. I had to brace myself to prevent from toppling over and crushing her.

Butterflies fluttered about in my stomach. "Are you sure?"

She bit down on her lower lip, making me wish that I could nibble it myself. That simple innocent action of hers had been driving me crazy every time she'd done it.

I felt her fingers around the belt loops to my jeans, forcing me lower.

Her lips brushed against mine. "This is your house, it's a big bed, and you're not sleeping on the couch."

I played with her hair and studied her. "It's not so bad."

"Pax?" Her gaze flittered between my mouth and eyes.

"Hmm?" I leaned toward her.

"Kiss–"

I never let her finish, knowing that we both wanted the same thing.

She ran her hands from my belt loops to around my hips

and under my shirt. The feather-like contact as her fingers traced about my lower back heated my flesh. She nibbled on my lip. Her soft tongue met mine as we sought closeness. She tasted sweet and I wondered what the rest of her would taste like, or if I'd be lucky enough to find out. Something told me that I was well on my way with the way things were heating up.

I let my hand wander from her side down to her hip. Her leg folded up at the knee, allowing me better access to squeeze her jean-clad cheek, causing her to moan into my mouth. I kissed the length of her jaw, down to the side of her neck, up to her ear.

"You have no idea how much I want you right now," I said.

Her body trembled.

I nipped her lobe, eliciting a whimper from her as her hands came free of my shirt and made their way to my hair. I felt the prickling of my scalp followed by a rush of arousal as she pulled.

My pants tightened further. If she had any question as to how much she turned me on, the vixen that lay beneath me had a feasible answer as I pressed my lower half into hers.

Alissa rolled us over and straddled my waist with a wry grin. "If you want something, Paxton, you've got to take it." She grabbed onto the hem of my shirt and I arched my back to help her remove it.

A look of hunger twinkled in her eyes as she studied my upper body. A finger ran up the middle of my stomach, starting at the waist of my jeans, circling my navel. The tickling digit changed to an open palm, which rubbed my chest as she leaned forward to bring her lips inches from mine.

I reveled in all things Alissa.

The woman was a temptress, a master at seduction, and she behaved as if she had no clue to her prowess. That hot and moist tongue of hers, mixed with her nips and the series of open-mouthed kisses heading down my torso, was wreaking havoc on my senses. An internal fight broke out between my urge to flip her over and exact my sensual revenge, and that of staying put to see where she was going to end up next.

Reduced to breathlessness, I managed, "Allie?"

Her fingers toyed with the button at the top of my jeans. Her mouth latched onto one of my nipples, flicking that wicked tongue of hers over the hardened disk. "Hmm?" The vibrations sent electrical currents throughout my body.

She leaned up to kiss my mouth. I felt her smile against my lips and saw the crinkling at her eyes when the button snapped out of its eyelet.

In that moment, something snapped in me also.

I flipped us over, grabbed her hands and pinned them above her head with one of mine. My other hand roamed free to find the exposed flesh around her stomach from her shirt riding up.

"Too many layers." I grunted my disapproval.

She helped me with stripping her shirt, and discarded it to the floor much like mine had been. I looked upon her as her blonde hair draped over my pillow, garnishing her head as if it were a halo. She looked delicious, and I was desperate to taste more than just her mouth.

"So soft," I said against the middle of her stomach while depositing soft kisses on my way up to those lace-covered mounds of hers.

I slid my hand underneath the band and took a breast in my hand, pinching its nipple and rolling it. She gasped and arched toward me.

Junior swelled to desperation in my jeans. I knew I'd have to at least unzip myself to allow for a bit of breathing room, and soon.

I pulled myself off of her and kneeled between her legs. Her face was flushed, her breathing was labored and her eyes… *Wow!* They were the brightest deep blue I had ever seen.

My hands reached for her fly and button. She tilted her hips up in permission and I pulled her denims off.

Damn! The woman sure knew her lingerie.

I grunted my approval at the sight of the matching black lace accentuating her slender, toned legs, and looking forward to the time they would be wrapped around me.

Amusement could be seen all over her face as she observed me taking her in.

"You look like a kid who's visiting an amusement park for the first time." Her voice had turned husky. "Your turn. Take off those pants, stud."

I mock saluted, gaining me a giggle while I proceeded to stand beside the bed and dropped *trou*.

Feeling her urge to stay close, she knelt on the edge of the mattress. Her palms met my chest; leaving a burning trail from the moment they made contact. Our eyes met and all playfulness, all mischievousness, was absent. In its stead, vulnerability dominated.

In that moment, I was reminded of Alissa's past relationship troubles. She knew of my hang-ups as much as I knew about hers. Honestly, she'd been the one to make me see that there was more to life than just existing. That there was someone out there that was better suited for me than my ex-wife ever had been.

Julie.

Talk about a proverbial bucket of iced water to cool things down a notch.

I need to tell her.

Here she was, single, hot and ready and even though she knew of my separation, I felt like a cheat.

A moron.

A liar.

Yeah, definitely a lying cheat of a moron.

night break

nightSHADE 1

CAREY DECEVITO

<u>P R O L O G U E</u>

D A L T O N

One Year Ago...

If I had to deliver that fucker's obituary, this is how it would read:

Rick Donnelly—Wannabe war hero, traitor, terrorist. May he burn in hell.

In truth, he was the scum who managed to kidnap my friend Theo Lowell's nephew, Jasper, then made off with the man's woman, all for the sake of petty revenge and furthering his stance in organized crime.

Now, he was nothing but a piece of shit, sprawled forward, split in half, and wedged between Warehouse Ten and the front end of Theo's brother's pickup truck.

Dead.

Collapsing to my back, Theo held onto his woman, Morgan, at my side. Allowing a long, drawn-out breath to escape, it helped ease the tension in my body as I dealt with the pain in my hand and leg. The damn bastard might be dead, but he did some damage before Morgan drove a truck straight through him. My shooting hand now had a hole through it, and since I was reaching for the gun in my ankle holster at the time, the fucking bullet managed to hit my bad knee.

It's over. Thank God for crazy-assed women, great friends…and random strangers.

Jasper was safe.

Morgan was safe.

And Theo could settle into the life he thought he'd all but lost only hours before.

Sounding on the verge of tears, he uttered, "Huss?"

With our adrenaline dropping from the night's festivities, I couldn't blame his emotional state. The same gamut of emotions was reeling through me too, and I hadn't had to track down two loved ones, nor had I had the displeasure of being held hostage, having to free myself, then do the same for the woman I loved. All this with some unknown cyber vigilante, who'd popped out of nowhere, to help him out. One we'd been forced to have blind faith in.

I'm your girl, Mr. T.

Yeah, Hussy was our girl tonight. Definitely.

"Yeah?" she said through that voice distorter of hers.

"Thank you." Theo's voice lodged in his throat, leaving the man incapable to add to his words.

It took a few seconds to get a response, but when it came, albeit in that robotically masculine voice again, it was just as overwrought with the same jumble of emotion that Theo and I seemed to be experiencing. "You're welcome, Mr. T," she whispered.

Hussy's earlier concerned outburst to my being shot jumped to the forefront of my mind. This spurred me into action. I didn't know why I felt compelled to reassure her, but I found myself unable to stop myself from doing it. Hussy wasn't one of my team at Nightshade Security, yet tonight, she had come through for all of us. Despite never having met, a bond had been forged between the team, Hussy, and myself. Plus, I've always been one to listen to my gut, and it's proven me right every time, so it was why I said what I did next.

"Huss?" I managed.

Her distorted voice caught. "Yeah?"

"I'll be fine." I swallowed the ball of emotion that had made my voice come out sounding like gravel. "But I'm going to need your name, honey."

What I got next was an unaltered, breathless sounding, "Kip," that made my lungs seize, my body tighten, and a part of my anatomy take notice in a very visceral way.

I had no idea who this woman was. She'd only spoken a single word—the nickname she'd given me based on my last name—Kippers. But that's all I needed. I can't explain the electrical charge that rolled through me, or the sense that something greater was at play. I simply needed more of that voice. I needed more of *her*. "I want to know—"

I heard a subtle thump on the other end of the line, followed by a long sigh.

I never thought that a sigh could hold so much untold emotion, but hers did.

Exhaustion.

Wistfulness.

Hesitation.

Defeat.

Fear.

"Don't," she whispered, and I could have sworn I'd heard her add a "please" to that. "Let's just leave it at this." I didn't want to. A gnawing feeling in my gut told me that I needed her still; that I wanted her. "I only did what needed to be done. It's what I do."

Something told me that pushing her right then would be ineffective, so I gave in, much to my displeasure. But I did it in a way that left the proverbial door open and the ball in her court. "Okay, Huss. If you ever need anything—"

I could tell that she was contemplating my words. "I won't." The tone of finality in those words had disappointment weighing me down until she continued, "Tell you what, I'll be in touch if something ever comes up."

Disappointment fled and hope took its place. This was as good as I was going to get. "Okay."

Silence dominated the next ten seconds before Hussy broke it. "I'm going to sign off now."

"Huss?" I was desperate and I didn't care. I wanted to reach through the communication device shoved in my ear canal and yank her to where I lay, so I could see the face that belonged to the voice. I wanted to figure out why she was how she was, what made her tick, what set her off. Hell, I'd have been happy to wait out the medics and the slew of first responders with her voice in my ear, telling me everything was going to be okay, just like Theo was doing with Morgan.

But before I could do or say anything, the line went dead, all coms were down, and sirens could be heard in the distance.

I could feel Theo's gaze aimed at the side of my face. He probably wanted to know what the fuck was going on with me.

Ignoring the man, I thumped my head onto the dock in sheer frustration, and closed my eyes. "Bye, Huss," I whispered.

CHAPTER 1

DEVOLIN

Come on. Come on. Come on!

"Come. *On!*" I bounced in place as I watched the progress bar run its course, and then punched the air in victory once it hit one-hundred-percent. "Gotcha!"

Disconnecting the thumb drive from my laptop, and slamming the top down on it, I scooted out of bed and proceeded to stuff the lot into my satchel.

There was no other option than to go straight to *him*.

This was life or death, and everything hinged on what I did next. I'd long since made a promise to myself that I'd never risk making contact with the team I'd bonded with after one night of mayhem. But promise or not, this information I'd just dug up wasn't something I could relay to him over the phone.

It needed to be seen.

Analyzed.

Discussed.

That meant that I needed to see Dalton Kippers. In the flesh. Talk to him. Show him what I'd found, what he was in for.

Then, I needed to get far away from him, and move on already, because this crazy obsession I had developed over the man was getting out of hand. My best friend, Skylar, had told me as much on multiple occasions. And when Skylar deemed it fit to force her wisdom upon me, I needed to listen. It's been nearly a year since I helped Dalton and his team rescue Jasper Lowell and Morgan Smyth for Christ's sake!

On a snort, I shrugged off where my thoughts were heading and closed my bag.

"What are you doing?"

The breath in my lungs seized. "Sky!" Hand clutched at my chest, I turned to face the woman, waiting for my erratic heartbeat to calm. "You scared the living shit out of me."

Skylar leaned against the doorjamb, dressed in wrinkled hot pink scrubs from a hard day's work, smirking. "Well, at least we know one of us is capable of getting that ticker of yours up above a slow trot now, don't we?" She breezed into the room, nodded toward my satchel, a glimmer of curiosity entering her gaze. "What's going on?"

I bit my bottom lip, knowing the guilt showed on my face for what I was about to ask of my dearest friend. Then I blurted, "Sky, I need your help."

"Do I need to worry that the cops will be coming in here to cart your ass off to jail?" she asked.

"I need to get out of here for a few hours."

"Dev, you know I can't—"

"It's life or death, Sky."

Skylar's eyes widened. "Dev, what in the hell have you gotten yourself into?"

I headed toward the cabinet, that passed itself off as a closet, and grabbed the pair of jeans and t-shirt I'd been wearing when I had been admitted. My irritation at the lack of immediate support showed with each jerky movement I made. "Can you or can't you help me out?" I turned to look at her from over my shoulder.

Skylar crossed her arms over her chest, taking a seat in the chair closest to my hospital bed. "You look flushed. How're you feeling, and tell me the truth."

Oh no, not that no-nonsense tone of hers. If I told my friend, who incidentally was a nurse, that I was feeling 'off' for lack of a better description, there'd be no way Skylar would let me walk out of there, say nothing of her covering for my absence with Doris, the nurse that was currently on duty. Damn woman was so old, she should have retired a decade ago, but seemed to find it amusing to torture her patients. That's why Skylar and I had dubbed her Nurse Battle-Axe. Because of this, and the fact that I did need to get out of there, I went with, "I'm fine," and hoped that my bad acting, let alone lying skills wouldn't give me away.

Unfortunately, the lack of conviction my words held, and the pause I had to take to brace myself against the wall to wait out the wave of dizziness that hit me, didn't help my cause.

"Uh-huh…"

"I'm not kidding, Sky. I need to do this." I whipped my pajama top off and flung it at the bed, slipping my shirt on. "This case…it's *big*."

"Dev—"

"No!" I persisted, yanking down my pajama bottoms, then headed to the bed for needed support. Leaning on it, I slid my legs into my jeans, wiggling them up over my ample hips. "*He*'s in danger, Sky."

Her eyes rounded as realization hit her. "He, as in *he*?" I nodded. "I thought we'd discussed this, Dev." She sighed.

"No, *you* discussed it. I merely listened. You told me to move on and I will. Just…" My frustration came out in a huff. "I have to see this through. It's my fault he took this case in the first place, so by default, it's my responsibility to make sure he knows what he's heading into. The people he'll be dealing with…" Another sigh accompanied my shake of the head. "They're not good, Sky."

"Okay." Skylar paused mid-thought. "Say I let you leave. How the hell am I supposed to keep Doris out of here?"

"She knows you come in here after your shifts. She never bothers to check in on me when you're here, you know that."

"So you want me to…?" She let her words hang so I could fill the gap.

"I know it's not right for me to ask this of you, but can you stay here, as in this room, until I get back?" Biting my lip in that nervous tick of mine, I continued, "And I'll need your keycard."

"Devolin!" she scolded.

Both of us looked toward the room's door and listened for a short moment to see if Skylar's outburst had generated some attention.

"I'll take the back way out and come in the same way. The emergency stairwell is just outside that door."

"I can get fired for that," she whisper-yelled, shooting the door another glance. Still, the woman pulled her access pass and handed it over.

I snapped it up from her hand then shrugged. "Just say you lost it if anyone asks."

"Yeah, yeah. You're lucky I love you, woman," she grumbled.

Knowing I had her where I wanted her, I grinned. "So you'll help me out?"

On a curt nod, Skylar got to her feet. "Yeah." Her eyes did a full head to toe appraisal before she shared my smile. "But we need to do something about your hair and makeup first."

I blew out a relieved sigh, hoping my eyes conveyed my appreciation. I really would have left against hospital advice—sure, I'd return after my duty was done—because a life, if not lives, hung in the balance and it was all my fault.

Sneaking out of my room, and down the stairwell, proved to be easy enough. Nurse Battle-Axe was out on the floor and away from the nurses' station. Heading down two floors, I exited the stairs, and made my way toward the bank of elevators that would take me the rest of the way down to the main lobby. When I got there, I jumped in the first cab that I spotted, rattling off my home address.

Upon my arrival, adrenaline running at an all-time high, I hurried to my vehicle. Finding it parked in its usual spot of my mother's garage, I noticed the bay next to it was empty and thanked the powers up above that I wouldn't have to deal with dear old Mom right away.

Hitting the fob, I opened the door, dropped my bag on the passenger seat, then settled into the driver's side.

"Hello, baby," I cooed to my newest acquisition, the leather upholstered finish and new car smell that had yet to fade, even after nearly a year of ownership.

Hitting the button that would open my bay's door from the controller on my visor, I put the key in the ignition and turned it. Sending my destination from my phone to the car's GPS, I took a few short seconds to enjoy the purr of the Charger's engine. Then I shifted my ride into reverse.

Nightshade Security Investigations—Dalton's company—was closed, so I made my way to the former corporal's home to find that it too lacked the one man I was trying to locate. I did take the time to admire the two rockers on his front wraparound porch and the American flag hanging in a place of pride on one of the support pillars framing the steps.

I hope I'm not too late.

I wasn't sure what I'd do if Dalton had already skipped town. Just as quickly as that thought popped into my head, another followed it.

Theo would know where he is.

Reprogramming my GPS for Theo and Morgan's place, I reared out of the drive and floored the gas pedal. Fifteen minutes later, my lead foot caused me to nearly miss the entry to the driveway, as I reached my third, and hopefully, final destination.

It wasn't until my finger released the doorbell that I realized how truly horrible I was feeling. To make matters worse, my nerves had also kicked in, and I had a fleeting thought that perhaps I should have given myself a quick cursory glance in the mirror before exiting the car. There were no do-overs on first meetings, after all, and I was about to meet more than just Theo and possibly Morgan today, seeing as it looked to be that they had a visitor, judging by the third vehicle parked at the front of the house.

As luck would have it, someone was home.

I would have cried out my relief at the sight of the pregnant woman before me, but a whispered, "Morgan," was the only thing I could muster as soon as the door opened.

The woman's eyebrows furrowed in apparent confusion. "Do I know you?"

I shook my head, indicating the negative, because that's all I could do. I was too busy fighting the sudden bout of nausea and dizzying heat. Next thing I knew, my vision tilted, then dimmed, and my knees gave out.

At the feel of a cool damp rag sponged against the hollow of my throat, over my forehead, my cheeks, and then back again, some of my faculties returned. The sensation was like heaven on my overheated skin. I sighed at the same time a, "Mr. T," escaped me.

"W-what, did she say?" I recognized Dalton's voice immediately. Unable to get my eyes to cooperate and open, I heard a thump come from right beside me, accompanied by the heat of another body warming the side of my torso.

"Danger…Kip," I mumbled, and then everything started to fade again.

Before I was able to embrace the darkness that swooped in, I felt the palm of Dalton's callused hand gently cup my cheek as he whispered, "Huss?"

CHAPTER 2

DALTON

With a lot of convincing to get the medics to allow me to be there, here I was, sitting in the back of an ambulance with who I suspected was Hussy, the cyber ghost I'd set Brycen to tracking in his spare time over the last year.

Her name: Devolin Payton Taylor. At least that's what the ID in her bag said when I managed to sneak a look at it after the paramedics had located it. I wouldn't be surprised if she'd faked her own identity, seeing as she seemed hell-bent on remaining anonymous.

Leaning forward onto my knees, I peered at the woman splayed out onto the gurney before me. Out cold.

Morgan had told me that Hussy looked panicked when she first opened the door to the woman. Then she'd collapsed and Theo had called 911. Morgan rushed to get me a cold cloth, and I'd been left with an unconscious woman. Her head rested in my lap, as I tried to decipher what her few short words meant, and why she'd chosen now to show herself.

Devolin whimpered in her sleep, causing me to reach out and grab the hand closest to me. Her very tiny, dainty, exceptionally soft hand.

My eyes trailed up from her digits, her arm, her shoulder, the delicate neck that held a thrumming but steady pulse, to her face. Her license said she had green eyes, but

I wondered if they'd shimmer like emeralds, taper closer to the hazel side of things, or would be bright like aquamarines. Beyond that, her lips were full, dark pink, almost rosy, reminding me of bubble gum. A fleeting curiosity of if she'd taste as such washed over me, but I shrugged it off. It was her hair that had me begging to set it free and run my fingers through it. It was a deep auburn, with streaks of darker reddish hues mixed in. Her skin was pale, but I knew, with the small line of freckles over the bridge of her cute nose, that her complexion wasn't that much darker when she wasn't ill, as she seemed to be now.

What the fuck is the matter with you? Scolding myself internally for waxing poetic about an unconscious woman, one I'd had a past with, yet had never met before. I bowed my head, trying to devise a plan of action, now that I had bullied my way into being by her side.

DEVOLIN

I woke up in what looked like the back of an ambulance, my hand clutched in a firm and warm grasp.

Allowing my head to drop sideways, I found myself looking at Dalton, who sat beside me. His head was bent forward. He was leaning onto his knees, one of them bouncing out of what I surmised was anxiety. I can only imagine what went through his, Theo's, and Morgan's heads when here I had shown up out of nowhere, and then before I could explain anything, I pulled a Sleeping Beauty maneuver on their asses. That thought had me rolling my eyes, cringing internally.

Dalton had yet to notice that I'd woken up, so I took the opportunity for a more thorough perusal of the unguarded man before me while I had it.

His dark brown, almost black hair was due for a cut,

slightly falling over his eyes. I wondered how it would feel between my fingers if I were to brush it away. Dalton had a chiseled jaw with a slight square shape, full lips, strong and masculine features that guaranteed him to look mean one minute, yet soft when the time called. His nose had a slight bend to it, most likely from combat, as with the small scar on the side of his right cheek, by his hairline. I could only assume since I'd been unable to access most but not all of his service records. He looked infinitely better in person than in any of the photos I'd dug up. Trust me, I'd searched those babies out, if only to indulge in my insane obsession over a man I've never met, but had spoken with once.

Damn!

Dalton must have sensed that I was conscious for his head shot up and his steel grey eyes connected with mine. "You're awake." The silk of his voice ran over me, goose-bumps exploding on my skin, making me withdraw my hand from his so I wouldn't give myself, or my reaction to him, away.

Double damn! Wait; was that my voice? Embarrassment filled me as a grin broke over his face, solidifying the fact that I had spoken aloud. But that look though… Had I felt anywhere close to one-hundred-percent, that look on his face would have melted my panties. I'm sure of it.

As it was, my mouth had gone dry, my tongue feeling as if it had tripled in size. "Uh."

"If you're going to look, I'd rather you be doing it while I can watch." His grin transformed into a smile.

My mouth opened for a rebuttal to his bold statement, then closed because words evaded me.

Light danced in the man's eyes. "The jig is up, Huss." His words were filled with pride. "Or should I say Devolin Payton Taylor?"

"How'd?" He patted my hand then twined his fingers

through mine, setting off another set of goosebumps, but I knew how he found out. "You went through my stuff."

He followed his curt nod with, "How are you feeling?"

I tried to pry my hand from his like before, but he didn't give this time. "Where's my bag? I—I need to show you something."

"I asked you a question, Devolin."

I pulled at my hand again. Stuck. "Just let me—"

Instead of the gentle tone he'd led with, this time, his words brokered no argument. All alpha-like. "Don't. Brush. Me. Off, Devolin."

"But—" My words ceased halfway out of my mouth as his lips formed a thin line in warning, his hand squeezing mine as an added measure.

I tried to lift my head, but collapsed back onto the stretcher's pillow as the nausea and dizziness, that had been absent since my waking, set in again. For the first time today, I started to really worry. This was all too reminiscent. Closing my eyes, I begged. *Please don't let it be back. I can't deal with this right now.*

"What is it?"

My eyes snapped open. The paramedics had to have given me drugs or something. It could be the only reason why I couldn't keep my thoughts to myself.

Dalton leaned closer, the squeeze on my hand a gentle one. "What's back? What's the matter? Come on, Dev, talk to me."

He couldn't know. I didn't want him to know. I was there simply because I felt responsible in warning him, to keep him and his team at NSI safe. I should have known that exploring my connection with Dalton couldn't lead to… And what was it that I wanted it to lead to? A happily ever after? I snorted at the thought then averted his questing gaze by turning my head to look up at the ambulance's ceiling. No, there would be none of that romance book nonsense for me. If I was having a relapse of some kind, this solidified why I had to push him away. I was best off making sure he had what he needed for that case of his; then disappearing from his life like I'd done the first go around.

Impatience clearly showing, Dalton groaned, "Devolin."

I closed my eyes, soaking in the warmth growing inside me, all due to the sound of his voice. Trying to breathe away my nausea, I silently prayed he'd say my name again. "You smell good. Like soap, mint, and man," I whispered.

"Devolin." He sounded humored.

I chose to ignore him, until I felt his other hand cupping my cheek. Then I couldn't.

Before I could react, deflect, possibly shove my foot in my mouth further, "Sir, we're at the hospital," came from one of the medics at the front of the vehicle. "We need you to clear out." The back door to the ambulance opened with the other attendant standing there.

"Wait!" I cried out as Dalton began to back out of the rig. "My bag!"

"What is it with you and that bag?" the man grumbled, and then lifted the messenger satchel to show me that it had been with us all along.

"Take it. There are things on the thumb drives that you need to see." The medics proceeded to unload my stretcher from the rig as Dalton stood at my side. "It's about the Wentworth case."

His body stiffened, eyes narrowing on me. "How do you know about that?" he clipped.

I wasn't about to apologize for doing what was right, even if he made me feel like a scolded child just then.

Showing my stubbornness, I jutted my chin up and said, "It doesn't matter. You need to do it right away." I'd be damned if something happened to him, or a member of his team, when I'd been the one to put them in this mess, all thanks to a personal connection.

"Fine. I'll get Brycen to meet me here, then you can show us what you've got when the doctor gives you the all clear."

"No!" Being around him was the last thing I needed. Hell, if working together on that one mission had caused me to lose my head about him, I feared what working with him and his team in person would do. "Just take it. Take the laptops and the thumb drives, too. There's more stuff on those. Brycen will know what to do with it. You won't need me. Just leave me my wallet. It's all I need that's in there."

The man got right in my face, anger, or was it exasperation, emanating from him. It caused me to jerk back into the stretcher's cushions. "You're not getting away from me this time, Devolin," he snapped, his nostrils flaring.

"That's not—"

"You two can do this later," the driver stated. "Miss Taylor, we need to get you back to your room and checked out."

"What?"

Ignoring Dalton's outburst, the medics wheeled me toward the hospital entrance.

CHAPTER 3

DALTON

I was fucking obsessed.

Years ago, I swore I'd never get like this over a woman again and now look at me. Taking that same old stroll down that same old road. Yet, despite how it turned out for me the first time around, here I was, spending the last year using my own company's resources to track down someone who would be deemed, by anyone with a functioning brain, a ghost.

From the moment the mission to rescue Theo's nephew and Morgan ended, White Hat Hussy had disappeared from the deep web, never to be seen or heard from again. Well...sort of.

It was bad enough that her voice has haunted me since *that* night.

The silky, smooth, low and sultry cadence, with a subtle Northern lilt, was never far from my mind. I heard it while out on missions. It was there again when I fell asleep.

Truth be told, I had no idea why, or how for that matter, this woman had infiltrated my thoughts. But random things reminded me of her. I found myself imagining what she looked like. I wondered how old she was, or if she thought of me as often as I did her.

It had been months since I'd seen sign of life from her. A year since I'd last heard her voice. The guys at

Nightshade Securities still gave me hell when I inquired if they'd turned anything up. They thought I'd fallen off my rocker. Maybe I had.

Then again, Devolin made it impossible to forget her.

When my ass landed in the hospital, after being shot, she sent me flowers. I'm not talking about one of those *get-well* bouquets, either. Hell, she'd gone overboard, embarrassing me in front of the others. Even Morgan, a florist for Christ's sake, asked me if I intended on becoming a rival of hers, what with every surface available—and some of the floor—being covered in vase after vase.

But Devolin, our little cyber angel, had gone the extra mile. I hadn't been the only one to suffer her wacky sense of humor, or been blessed with her generosity.

With Shane, she'd help close a bunch of cases that had either gone cold or lacked information to proceed with their current lead. For Morgan and Theo, she'd sent the man a *Mr. T* doll, and a few other more meaningful gifts in celebration of their nuptials. Hell, Brycen might not have thought of it as funny at the time, but the rest of the guys from that night, myself included, thought it was hilarious how she'd infiltrated the computer wiz's system, repeatedly, only to leave dancing babies for him to find. Shit, even Theo's nephew hadn't been left untouched. Jasper had a custom blanket delivered to him, with each one of us guys' names on it. The note it came with, typed up mind you, commended him on his bravery. She also told him that if things ever got scary again, all he had to do was hide under the blanket and that he'd be safe.

Each gift or act had thought put into it. Maybe that's why I was hung up on her, I don't know. Which is why, with every delivery, I pushed the guys to track her down.

But each box or envelope lacked the return address they needed. And forget fingerprints. Each service utilized had no way of providing the billing information, or any information for that matter, because she'd gotten into their systems to erase the data. Items were paid for in cash. The surveillance systems were of no help either. The damn woman had thought of everything to make sure she stayed incognito.

Yet, now I'd found her.

Technically, she found you, dumbass.

And by the looks of things, she wasn't doing very well. So naturally, when a nurse approached me, volunteering to show me to the waiting room, I followed her.

It wasn't until my ass landed in a seat of the Chronic Care Ward, that worry hit me. About the same time it did, so did my stubbornness.

If Devolin thought she could get rid of me, she was mistaken. I'd sit there and wait for as long as it took until I could get to her. I didn't want answers on the Wentworth case from what Brycen could find on her devices. I wanted answers straight from the source. Devolin.